MISTLETOE KISSES

NANA MALONE

1

NOMI

My office had exploded in Christmas cheer. Indeed, Everywhere I turned there was tinsel and mistletoe and Christmas lights.

It wasn't like I hated the holidays. But when you grew up where I did and your entire town was known for their Christmas celebrations, you got tired of some of the pomp and circumstance. Never of the eggnog though.

I really did love eggnog.

But I never really enjoyed Christmas. My mother was always working. And my father was never really in a celebratory mood. So even though we had the tree, the trimmings and all those things, I knew my mother had a whole other family she would be with most of the holiday. So I never really enjoyed it.

Not to mention, the holidays in California just didn't feel like the holidays. Palm trees were not exactly festive. I didn't care how many times and ways you decorated them. And without the precursor of fall, Christmas just felt, hollow.

Nevertheless, my office always did it up for the holidays. It was as if no one could possibly fathom that there might be someone who didn't love the holiday season. Once Halloween was over, the office exploded in Christmas cheer.

The meeting alert went off on my laptop. I scooped it up, unplugged it and grabbed the mug my assistant had gotten me. The mug read "Save a horse, ride a reindeer." The reindeer happened to look an awful lot like Ryan Gosling wearing reindeer ears.

I wasn't mad at it, but still.

Ella had given it to me two years ago. And last year when I hadn't used it because I'd shoved it in a drawer somewhere, she'd looked sad. Not that she said anything, but she really wanted me to use it.

This year, I hope she kept it simple and got me a gift card or something. I liked gift cards. They were practical and useful.

You really are a Scrooge.

I was not a Scrooge. I liked to give presents. I liked getting each person the perfect thing that they needed. Or didn't even know that they needed until they had it. I just could have done without all the ...well, Christmas.

My managing editor, Brianna Foster, called to me down the hall. "Hurry up Nomi. We need an update."

"I'm on my way."

Brianna liked everyone to feel like they were family. So instead of pitch meetings being held in the conference room, we all piled into her office. We sat on the comfy couches and kicked off our shoes. During the holiday season, she served hot toddies. Even though it wasn't cold outside. Not that I would turn down a hot toddy, but still. I dutifully extended my mug at the door and Ella grinned when she saw it. She poured me my portion and I took a seat near Brianna.

All I wanted to do was get our next issue out, and then I would be on vacation. Two solid weeks of bliss. I was headed to the Bahamas. Solo no less. I planned to be like Stella and get my groove back.

Are you hoping there'll be a Taye Diggs in the islands?

Let's just say I wasn't opposed to meeting someone. But mostly, I just wanted a break. I'd been going hard for the last several years and if everything went well this time around, I would have my promotion, take my vacation, and come back and hit it hard.

Oh yeah, that doesn't sound lonely at all.

Most of the update meeting went fine. Kyle gave us the advertising numbers for the issue; we already had the frontpage story. Everything was going well until the subject came around to Nolan Polk.

Ella fidgeted in her seat in her ugly Christmas sweater that had a Santa that lit up the phrase ho ho ho and blinked. Santa was also riding a sleigh. And Rudolph's nose was also blinking bright red. "I'm so sorry to tell you this. We can't find Nolan Polk. So far, the only word we've had from his agent, is that he's not interested."

What the hell? Nolan Polk was the center peace of our whole cover story. "What do you mean he said no?" I asked and stared at Ella.

Ella shook her head. "I'm sorry Nomi. I've tried everything. His agent, Ronyelle, his Facebook page. Hell, I even hired someone, and *they* can't find him. The guy is a ghost. The only thing I've been able to dig up is that he lives in some place called Faith, VA."

My heart stuttered. *Oh hell.*

Brianna, sat forward. "Didn't you grow up in Faith, Nomi?"

I swallowed hard and locked my jaw. Just thinking about my hometown was enough to make me ill. "Yeah, but I haven't been back in a long time."

Brianna sat back. "What do you suggest we do? This twentieth anniversary special edition is supposed to be epic. You turned us on to this guy and he's perfect for the theme of beauty around the world. We have to find him."

The whole table looked at me for guidance. Four years ago, Nolan Polk had burst onto the photography scene and become a media darling with an anti-bullying campaign he'd done with *Rolling Stone Magazine.* They'd done a photo call, looking for up and coming photographers. After that he'd been extremely prolific. Everyone had wanted him. And then two years ago, he mysteriously stopped producing, only donating the occasional photograph for charity. It made him a hot commodity.

Unfortunately, he was also notoriously reclusive. *Sassy Magazine* had been angling to get him to do a spread since he popped onto the scene. A photo from him would be the perfect addition to our twentieth anniversary lineup. Though, that was only *if* we could get him. And that meant finding him first.

I twirled my pen and tried to steer the direction of the conversation. "I think we should put a private investigator on it. We don't have much time. If his agent can't persuade him, then we either need to find another photographer or get someone down there. I might know someone who could look into it for us."

Ella shifted in her chair. "I mean, I've tried everything. I even had our people in New York go down to his agent's apartment to try to negotiate. No luck. Maybe his representation is out of town."

Or maybe Nolan Polk didn't *want* to be found.

It wasn't in my nature to back down from a challenge. Okay, not exactly true. I'd once run away from home and hadn't looked back on what I'd left behind, ever. But I was a whole new person now. The kind of person who got things done. "I'll get someone to Faith."

Brianna shook her head. "I think for something this important, *you* need to go yourself. I mean you are from there after all."

Wait, what? No, way, no how. "I'm sorry, what was that?"

Brianna pursed her lips as she always did when she was about to school someone. "You're from there. You know the locals. How hard will it be to ferret out one guy? You can do that in your sleep."

My skin went cold. I could do this.

No. No you can't. You can't go home to Faith. "Well, I mean it's the holidays and everything so I'm thinking there is a good chance even if I can track down where he lives, he won't be there." Not to mention that Faith was one of those towns that exploded during the Christmas holiday. See earlier about how I lacked Christmas cheer.

"Nomi, this is what we need right now. Can you commit to getting the job done?" Brianna asked.

Amber Divine leaned forward, her perfectly curled red hair bounced. "I can go if Nomi doesn't want to. I'm more than happy to be a team player." The way she said my name set my teeth on edge. I only let Brianna and Ella call me Nomi in the office. But I wasn't going to have that battle now. Amber was trying to get under my skin.

The two of us had been in the running for a Senior Editor position for months. If I let Amber go back to Faith and my competition got the Nolan Polk picture, the promotion I wanted so badly would go to her.

My boss tapped her pen against her lips. "Actually, that's not a bad idea. Having more boots on the ground will help."

Ella leaned forward. "I can have you guys on the first plane out in the morning to Richmond and scheduled to even come back before the holiday. From Richmond, you'll just need to grab the train to Faith, Nomi, but you know that. I know how you feel about Christmas, you'll be in and out."

"I really think it would be better to hire someone. Like a professional. Amber doesn't know the area and we'd be looking for a needle in a haystack." I squeaked. I hated the idea of Amber doing what I couldn't.

Or won't.

Couldn't. I decided. After everything, there was no way I could go back home.

Brianna frowned. "Why do I get the impression you don't want to do this Nomi?"

Because I don't. "Of course I do. I'm just worried we won't find him there during the holiday."

"Then let's hope you find a lead quick, because you're both heading to Faith."

I slumped in my chair. If I was going home, then I needed some reinforcements. And I'd have to make some arrangements. Ella was good at her job, but she didn't know Faith. Tourists started pouring into the town right after Thanksgiving and didn't let up till the New Year. It made hotels and car rentals to tool around town a nightmare.

As soon as the meeting was over, I trudged to my office and made a phone call I never thought I'd be making. At the same time, I started an online search for a rental car and hotel. The Resplendence Inn seemed to have rooms, so I sent the link to Ella to book. But so far I'd struck out on a car rental. And Faith wasn't exactly bustling with ride share companies. If push came to shove I could taxi it, but everyone knew everyone's business in Faith. There would be no hiding if I did that.

And then, I called the one person who could calm me down. Also, she happened to be the only person who knew why I hated Faith. After three rings, a harried Jilly Porter answered the phone. "This is Jilly."

I exhaled slowly. There was something comforting about my best friend's voice. "Hey girl, it's Nomi."

"Nomi! Honey, it's been two months since we talked! Why is that?"

She was right. It had been two months. I kept meaning to call her every weekend. But then I got embroiled in work and then it was too late to call. "I'm sorry. That's my bad. I text you every other day though."

"That's not the same and you know it." Leave it to Jilly to call me on my shit.

"Listen, we'll keep this short and save a big update for when I come home."

There was a breath of silence on the line. then, an ear-piercing squeal. "You're coming home? When?"

"Tomorrow. Any chance you can grab your girl from the train station?"

"You just tell me what time and I will have a ride for you. Probably Linc." She cursed then. "Damn it, I wish I could chat, but I'm getting stuff ready for a shipment. Here, talk to Linc."

My brain stuttered as she handed the phone off; "Long time no speak, stranger?"

The voice I remembered wasn't the one on the line now. When had his voice gotten so deep? From the time I moved to Faith, Jilly and I had been inseparable. Which meant that everywhere we went, Linc hadn't been far behind. He and Jilly ran in the same circles at school, but I could never say I knew him that well. Even though he'd also been best friends with my ex.

He'd never said much. But I'd always found him unsettling. Like I was always hyper aware of his presence. And Linc was more watchful than anything. He'd never needed to be the center of attention. And he'd helped get us out of more than a few scrapes thanks to my big mouth and Jilly's impulsive nature.

Although, I couldn't explain it, I always got the impression that he didn't like me. Maybe because he always looked so angry when I was around.

"Uh, Linc, hi. It's Nomi. Naomi Adams from Faith?"

There was a beat of silence. Then another beat. When he spoke again, his voice was low and raspy. "You honestly think I'd forgotten you? Without you, Jilly probably would have ended up as a rock star groupie or worse."

He had no idea how close he was with his teasing guess. Jilly and I had once snuck out to go to a Foo Fighters concert and Jilly had been hell bent on getting backstage by any means necessary, including flashing the bouncers her boobs if she had to. I had barely managed to talk her out of it.

"Listen, I'm sorry to impose, but Jilly volunteered you to pick me up at the train station tomorrow night. I know it's an inconvenience, but I can't seem to get a single rental car in the area."

"Yeah, the holiday rush is in full swing." His voice was warm and mellow, like melting chocolate. "Not to worry. It's cool. Just text Jilly the details and I'll be there."

Good ol' Linc. "Thank you. It's much appreciated. I'll owe you one."

"I'll hold you to it." There was a beat of silence, then he said, "Last time I saw you, you said you were never coming back to Faith."

Yeah, I had said that. And I'd meant it. "Apparently, never say never. I need to come back for work."

"You work for a magazine now, right?"

I had no idea why, but just talking to him made me a little nervous, my skin started heating. *It must be the voice.* It made it easy for me to forget I was talking to Jilly's brother.

"Yeah. They're sending me back to find Nolan Polk. He's supposed to live in Faith."

There was a long beat of silence. "What do you need him for?"

"Well, it's our twentieth anniversary edition and we're looking for some of his photos for a spread."

"I don't get it. Wouldn't you normally call his agent or something? I assume a guy like that has an agent?"

"Yeah, tried that. No luck. She isn't responding to our requests. So anyway, it appears I'm headed home to try and find him."

Linc's voice was soft, quiet. "Well, if anyone can find him, it's probably you. You always had a way of coming out on top."

I swallowed hard as my brain conjured up an image of myself on top of Linc, back arched in bliss. *What the hell was wrong with me?* Just because his voice was all grown and sexy didn't mean he'd grown with it. If he didn't like me then. He sure wasn't going to love me now.

"I owe you one Linc. I've got a lot riding on this."

His voice dropped an octave. "Oh, I plan on collecting Nomi."

2

LINC

Naomi Adams was coming home. When I hung up, I leaned my head back against the wall and shut my eyes tight. Caught somewhere between elation and dread, my brain tried to make sense of what she'd said. I'd had a thing for Nomi since she'd moved to Faith, but she'd never noticed me. She'd always treated me like a brother. Then she went out with my idiot best friend, and I'd lost my shot. Back then even though I never told her how I felt, it still felt like betrayal that she chose him. I may or may not have had a chip on my shoulder about it.

"You should look happier. *Why* don't you look happier?" Jilly asked.

I peeled an eye open to glare at my twin sister. She matched me in coloring, from her inky black hair to her jade green eyes. Her features were softened, more feminine versions of mine, down to the slight dimple in her chin. The only dissimilarity was the foot difference in height. She liked to tease that I'd stolen all her height genes. "That was low, Jilly. You should have given me some warning."

"Now why would I want to do that? Besides, are you going to pretend that you don't *want* to see Nomi?"

"I don't know what you're talking about." I said as I handed her back her phone. At times like this, I regretted the two of us being so close. It was impossible to hide anything from her.

"Bull. Eight years is a long time to hold a torch for someone, little brother."

"You're only older by a minute, Jilly."

She slid me a sideways glance. "What? You thought you were slick back then? Come on, for the most part you were pretty shy, but the moment Nomi was around, you had to peek out of your little shell and hang around. Not to mention you were pea green with envy once she started dating numb nuts."

I pinned a narrow-eyed gaze on my sister. Lucky for me, I'd outgrown that shy awkwardness and I'd filled out. No one would call me awkward and skinny now. But eight years *was* a long time. The last time I'd seen Nomi, she'd been running for the first train out of town after Brad cheated on her with Lila Banks, and chose the Banks money and connections, over her.

"Did you tell her?"

Jilly's brow furrowed. "What? No! I was hoping you would get up the balls and do it yourself. But I guess you never did."

The night she'd run away, Nomi had turned up at our house looking for Jilly to give her a ride. But my sister hadn't been there. Nomi had walked the two miles over from the country club in the rain after Brad had dumped her and she'd been soaked through.

When she asked me to swing by her house so she could grab her stuff and then take her to the train station, I hadn't tried to talk her out of it. Maybe because it hadn't hit me till we were on the platform that she was actually leaving. My stomach still knotted whenever I remembered what I'd said to her then. "You always deserved better than him."

And then like a fool, I'd kissed her.

I was pretty sure I'd fumbled my way through it. I'd made out with girls, but none I really cared about. And Nomi had been everything I wanted.

Jilly snapped her fingers in front of my eyes. "Earth to Linc. Did you hear me?"

I'd been too lost in my last memory of Nomi. "No. Sorry."

My sister rolled her eyes. "Focus. She's coming back, so what are you going to do about it?"

"Pick her up from the train station."

"Please don't be obtuse. This is your chance."

I knew what she meant. "She's only staying a couple of days, Jilly."

"I know, but that in itself is huge. She hasn't been home in eight years. Maybe you can convince her to stay a little longer. I don't know, maybe have a Christmas fling?"

A fling? Just the thought made my skin hot and itchy. But then what was new. Nomi had always made me feel that way. But she'd been off limits because she'd been dating my douche of a best friend. So, I'd shoved down any feelings I had for her and pretended she annoyed me.

Like a fool.

"It's not that easy, Jilly. She's coming back for Nolan Polk."

Jilly's eyes grew wide and she cursed under her breath. "What are you going to do?"

That was the question. I'd created the Nolan Polk pseudonym for my work back in college when I'd been trying to distance myself from the family name. I'd wanted people to want my work because it was good, not because my father was a senator. However, one bad decision and Polk had become a prison I couldn't escape.

There was no way in hell I would be able to help her find

Nolan Polk. Problem was, when Nomi had something she wanted, she wouldn't let it go.

"I can't use the Polk name or distribute that work until the New Year. If I do, I'm in breach and it'll cost me everything."

Jilly ground her teeth. "I could kill that woman for locking you into this deal."

I wished I could wipe my whole relationship with Melanie Stanfield off the plane of existence. Just thinking about it made anger pulse in my veins. When Melanie and I had been together, at first things were great. She had art connections thanks to her family, particularly, abroad. When I'd proposed, she'd officially become my agent.

The one clause in my contract I should have paid closer attention to stated that no one else could distribute my work for profit for a term of three years. At the time, I'd been convinced of our love. *Like a chump.*

But then things had gone bad. And she'd started paying more attention to the value of my work than the value of our relationship. When we'd broken up, she'd held me by the balls to my contract. *I'd rather eat glass than give her another dime.*

For the last two years since I'd been home, I hadn't sold or exhibited a single piece, except for charity. Suddenly the only thing I'd ever wanted had a hundred and ten pound blonde albatross attached to it.

But I'd made my bed and had to lie in it. "My fault, Jilly. I trusted the wrong person. I'm not eager to do that again."

Jilly shook her head. "Nomi wouldn't hurt you, Linc. That's not her."

No, that wasn't the Nomi I remembered, but I'd been wrong about people before. "I thought the same thing about Melanie once too."

My sister put a hand on my shoulder. "Maybe this gig could put you back on the map again. Have you shooting. This is your chance to finally leave for good. Maybe go back to Europe. See more of Africa. You always used to talk about it."

"That was a long time ago, Jilly."

She pursed her lips. "Sooner or later, you won't have Dad as an excuse anymore. You'll have to face the big bad world. You were destined for great things, little brother. Time to stop hiding."

I ignored the numb feeling that spread from the center of my chest. With our father's early onset Alzheimer's diagnosis two years ago, I'd come home to help out. Both Jilly and I had. For me though, it had also been a way to escape all the mistakes I'd made.

Though, coming home hadn't been any easier. My father had been a man's man. Confident, a little brash, but fair and kindhearted. It had helped him get elected to the senate over and over again. It had helped people trust him. That man was gone now. And it hurt. Some days weren't so bad, the lucid days. Which were still more than the non-lucid days. But the non-lucid days, the ones where my father couldn't even recognize me? Those hurt. Knowing he needed me was the sole reason I stayed. Otherwise, I'd have left off for parts unknown by now, spreading my wings. At least that's what I liked to tell myself.

"You wouldn't understand."

"Whatever you say. What I do know is, all you have to do to get the girl of your dreams is to share a part of yourself. It's not that hard Linc. Now's your chance to take a shot. Even if it's just for a couple of days."

First things first. Despite what I'd said, I needed to make sure Nomi never found Nolan Polk.

3

———

NOMI

I t was official. Hell had frozen over. And it looked an awful lot like Faith, Virginia. I strode through the train station looking around at the white canvas outside. Of course it was snowing. This was Virginia, after all, and there were only a few days left until Christmas. What did I expect? The balmy seventy-degree weather from Los Angeles looked mighty good right about now.

Get in and get out and you can go back.

I was giving myself three days to get what I needed and be back at home in the safety of my apartment.

I turned on my phone and checked my messages. I'd turned it off to preserve the battery since I was the idiot who had packed my charger in my suitcase and not my purse. So far nothing from Linc. Hopefully he was already here. I was behind the curve as it was. Amber had changed to an earlier flight, and presumably had caught the afternoon train, so I was playing catch up.

I took the escalator down, choosing to walk rather than ride it. All the while scanning the luggage area for Linc. Frowning when I didn't see him, I craned my neck. *Dumbass, he might have changed in all this time.*

The last I'd seen him, his dark hair had dusted his shoulders and he'd been rail thin and barely taller than me at maybe five feet nine inches if I was being generous. I had no idea what to picture now. Maybe he'd gone extra emo like every other hipster I knew and had grown a beard or a mustache to be ironic.

As I looked around, the memories of the last time I'd been home washed over me. When I'd left here eight years ago, the plan had been to never come back.

Thanks to my AP courses and the summer sessions I'd taken at the local community college, I had finished all my high school credits just before the Christmas holiday and planned to work from December through graduation and then head for UCLA in the fall. Brad was supposed to move with me and had been planning on attending the University of Southern California. That night at the country club had changed everything.

When he'd picked me up, he'd taken me to the big lake by the country club. Over the summers, there were usually parties out there, bonfires on the tiny beach. It was also the standard make out spot. But he hadn't taken me there to make out. Or hell, propose like my idiotic seventeen-year old self had thought.

Just thinking about what he'd said made my blood boil. "Naomi, it's been a fun two years, but we need to think about our futures. Or rather, I need to think about *my* future."

I had been too shocked to cry in the moment. And since I didn't say anything, he'd continued.

"As great as you are, you're not the right person to take into my future. I need to be with someone who compliments me. Someone who has the same vision."

What he'd meant was: someone with a rich family and even richer connections. For the most part, his parents had been okay with me. His mother was more disapproving of my middle-class roots than the fact I was black. But she'd never missed an opportunity to parade rich, blonde debutants in front of Brad. The ass wipe had finally taken notice. His next words still sat with me today. "I'm seeing Lila Banks now."

I had finally managed to find my voice then. "Lila Banks? That debutant barely has one brain cell."

"Well, she's perfect and her family is perfect. And Georgetown is a better school than USC. You don't really fit into my circles. And let's face it, not everyone would understand our relationship. You're the only one who didn't see this coming."

"H-how long?" I'd never regretted a question more.

"A few weeks. I'd have told you sooner. But your dad, implied my history grade would be in jeopardy if I hurt you before finals." I could still visualize his strong shoulders as they shrugged. "So, I waited until after the report cards had been sent."

Even now, I could remember the instant nausea when he'd said that. My parents had known. They could have insulated me or protected me, and they hadn't said a word. That verbal slap had left scars.

Brad had been with me only as a note of rebellion, but now that real life was starting, he wanted his perfect blonde girlfriend and perfect life, and I just didn't fit.

I walked away from him, leaving him at the top of the hill. Tears streaming down my face, I walked across the golf course and through the trails to Jilly's house. Somewhere along the way it had started to rain, the frozen splashes stinging my face as I walked.

Jilly hadn't been home, Linc had. He'd opened the door and dragged me inside by the fire and wrapped a blanket around my shoulders. After a change of clothes, a round with Jilly's blow dryer and some hot cocoa, I felt a little better.

He hadn't asked me anything, he had merely been there.

Linc hadn't batted an eyelash when I asked for a ride home so I could pack. His only objection was when I asked for a ride to the train station and that was that I should wait for Jilly to come back before I left. But my friend was at Villanova visiting the college and I just wanted out so bad I couldn't wait.

I will never forget Linc's last words to me. "You always deserved better than him."

"Yeah, I guess I see that now."

"You should have seen it before," he whispered. And that was when Lincoln did the one thing I'd never expected him to do.

Slanted his lips over mine and gave me the kind of kiss I'd only read about. But just as suddenly as it started, he stopped. The both of us stood there breathing harshly, my mind a swirl of confusion, awakening desire, and surprise.

But I didn't have any time to react. Because the conductor made the last call and I had to go. That was the last time I saw Linc.

Before that kiss, I'd assumed he didn't like me. I'd always seen him just as Jilly's brother. But I always liked him. Unlike most of the other kids at school, he'd talked to me when Brad wasn't around. But in that pestering brother kind of way. I always assumed it was because mom worked for his father but, given that he was braving the cold to come pick me up now, maybe I was wrong about him not liking me.

When I didn't see him, I shuffled to the baggage claim wishing I had worn Uggs instead of the Cole Haan stiletto boots. I opted to check my bag instead of lugging it from car to car. The train from Richmond had carried the usual commuter crowd, so the claims area was practically empty even though there were plenty of people waiting for their passengers.

For the most part, no one paid me any attention, but after several minutes, the hairs on the back of my neck stood at attention. Nervously, I whipped around, and expected to see someone behind me. There was no one there. However, at the far corner of the arrivals area, a man stood and stared right at me. He was tall, maybe around six feet or so. He had one of those thin, rangy builds that screamed soccer player or some sort of athlete. His dark hair curled over his forehead and framed one hell of a face. *Holy hell.* There were men that hot in Faith? Maybe I had been missing out.

Nervously I turned back and dragged my roll along off the miniature luggage carousel.

My neck still prickled with awareness. *Oh geez, was he staring?* I hazarded another glance over my shoulder. This time when our eyes met, the corner of his lips tipped up in a hint of a smile and my insides flipped.

No. No. No. I was not getting distracted by some hottie. I had a job to do. Tall-dark-and-rip-your-clothes-off over there was a dime a dozen in Los Angeles. Granted, the ones in LA were also pompous ass hats for the most part but still.

I turned back around to keep from staring some more, pulled up Linc's contact info on the phone and sent a quick text.

Hey, are you still okay to pick me up?

His reply came quickly. *Yeah. I'm already here.*

My brows snapped down. *Had I missed him?* The station had slowly thinned out. Despite my brain's commands to not look at the guy in the corner, I couldn't help a furtive glance. He smiled at me then and something pulled low in my belly this time, making me ache.

Oh hell. I have never been the one-night-stand type, but for that smile, I'd give it some serious consideration. *Focus, Nomi.* I turned my attention back to my phone.

Where are you? What are you wearing?

The suggestive nature of the text didn't hit me until I had

already sent the message. *Aww hell.* I had been home all of five minutes and was already a hot mess.

He was slower to respond now. *Dark jeans. Dark jacket... And I'm waving.*

This time when I looked up my jaw went slack. Tall-dark-and-turns-good-girls-bad was waving.

Pushing off the wall, he sauntered over with one of those panty-dropping smiles. As he got closer, my heart hammered faster and faster; I was certain I was having a heart attack.

He paused just in front of me. "I guess you didn't recognize me?"

Still slack jawed, I stared up at him and catalogued his face. His jade green eyes were dark and reminded me of the forest after a heavy rainfall. The cleft in the chin that had only been hinted at when we were kids was more defined. His angled jaw and chiseled cheekbones, combined with full sensual lips meant Lincoln Porter had turned into a full-blown hottie.

Speak. Close your mouth, swallow, and then find some intelligent words. The brain's commands were sound, but all I managed was, "Linc?"

He chuckled. "Yeah." He ran a hand over his hair. "It's me. I guess I look a little different."

"Understatement of the year."

The smile was back.

I couldn't help myself when I said, "I wonder if you still taste the same?"

4

LINC

She wondered if I tasted the same? The hot flush in my chest had nothing to do with embarrassment. I'd spent two years kicking myself for never saying anything, so I'd taken my shot.

Today though, Nomi hadn't recognized me. What the hell was I supposed to make of that? Okay, fair enough, the summer before college, I did add three inches to my frame and packed on some muscle finally when I'd started doing martial arts My mother always told me I would grow into my looks. *But I never expected Nomi to walk right by me.*

More dangerously, I wanted to know what she thought. I'd seen her appraising gaze as it slid over me, but from a distance it was hard to tell.

She swallowed hard. "Sorry. You just look so..." her voice trailed, but even in the bad lighting of the station, I saw her pupils dilate. With her lips parted ever so slightly, I wanted to take her photograph.

Yeah, not gonna happen. The moment she found out I was Nolan Polk, she'd take what she needed and bolt. And I did not want to go through that again. "It's good to see you, Nomi. You look good."

She wore her hair in slim braids that hung down her back. Her smile, now, that was the same. Her lips naturally curved upwards, making her look like she was always on the verge of laughter or mischief. She hadn't changed at all. Still slim, but her curves had filled in and made me itch to touch. Her cinnamon skin gleamed. And her wide, dark, almond-shaped eyes missed nothing.

She was still beautiful. *And likely still hung up on Brad Lennox so get your mind right, Linc.*

I cleared my throat. "C'mon, let's go get you settled." I picked up her bag and pulled it along.

"Must we?" she mumbled under her breath.

The comment made me chuckle. Acerbic wit was still intact. "I see you're no fonder of this place than when you left it."

Nomi shrugged. "I always knew you were astute."

Oh yeah, she hadn't changed. Problem was, neither had I, so she still had the power to make me a little nervous. "So, if you hate it so much, then what are you doing back here? At Christmas time no less. Surely someone else could have come. I seem to recall you saying you'd rather have your fingernails torn out."

"Hey, the night is still young." With a small laugh she added. "Hopefully, I'll be in and out. If my career trajectory didn't depend on it, I wouldn't be here encroaching on your Christmas holiday."

Once at my BMW, I unlocked and opened the passenger door for her, then deposited her bag in the trunk before sliding behind the wheel.

"You're not encroaching, Nomi. I'm happy to help. And since you won't be able to rent a car anywhere in a thirty-mile radius, I can take you anywhere you need to go." This situation wasn't ideal. The last thing I wanted her to do was find out I was in fact Nolan Polk, at least until I was sure she could be trusted. This way I could find out what she was really after.

She turned in her seat to study me. As her gaze slid over my face, I had to bite back the sudden compulsion to kiss her. She always had that unnerving way of looking at someone directly, clear to the soul.

"You seriously don't need to do that. I can manage."

"Independent to the bone. But be reasonable. You'll need help. I'm offering."

"I" Nomi shook her head. "Honestly, I don't even know what I'm looking for. You'd be signing up for what amounts to a wild goose chase."

There was no way I was letting her roam around asking questions. Not so much for the fact that I feared she'd actually find anything, but more so that I wanted to keep her close. Maybe Jilly was right, and she was the same old Nomi, and I could trust her. Then again maybe she cared more about her bottom line than anything else. The only way to know was to keep her close.

"Look, I get it. You like to do everything on your own. But help from a local can't be a bad thing."

"I don't want to keep you from anything. I'd feel terrible. And it's the holiday. I'm sure you have family obligations? A girlfriend? Somebody is going to need you. I got this."

My breathing slowed. Did she just ask if I had a girlfriend? "Right now, *you* need me. Family is fine and no girlfriend. Why can't you just accept help?"

She ducked her head. "I guess I've never been very good at it. I'd rather cut off my left boob."

Only with a Herculean effort did I manage to keep my gaze from flickering to her chest. "Can't have that now, can we?

Besides, my mother and Jilly would have my hide if I didn't help you. You're practically family." *Shit, way to put it out there.*

She blinked. "Uh, whatever the reason, I appreciate it. And any return favor, just name it."

"Am I taking you to your parent's house?"

She shook her head vehemently. "God no. I haven't seen either of them in a year and birthday conversations were awkward enough without me being under their roof. Besides, I'm not staying for the holidays so there's really no point of letting them know I'm here."

"So where to if not your parents'?"

"Resplendence Inn," she said absently.

Why there? That was the most expensive hotel in town. Vacationing celebrities looking for a Norman Rockwell Christmas had put Faith on the map. The town had become a booming tourist destination and with that had come development. Resplendence was one of the newer boutique hotels. "Nice place." Maybe she'd made all her dreams come true like she always talked about.

She shrugged. "The magazine booked it."

"So, what exactly do you want Nolan Polk for?"

Her morose mood lifted the second she started talking about her job. "*Sassy Magazine* is having our 20th anniversary issue and we're doing a women in beauty spread. But not like the usual bullshit stuff that the other magazines do of overly air-brushed celebrities that don't even look like themselves. Or just the western esthetic. We wanted to capture real women from around the world. This Polk guy, you should see his work. He does the most moving and intimate candid portraits. I think you'd like his stuff. You used to be into photography if I remember correctly?"

Used to. "Yeah. I dabbled."

She narrowed her gaze. "You more than dabbled from what I

remember. Didn't you win a competition or two? Jilly said you travelled a lot. I just always thought you'd travel the world taking pictures."

And I had. Or at least that was before I'd had my heart ripped out and had come home to lick my wounds. "Well, funny thing is, there is no place like home." The last thing I wanted was for her to dig further about my past, so I changed the subject. "So what? You lost your artist?"

"I didn't lose him, exactly. He just doesn't want to be found. Little does he know, I don't give up on anything. Ever. And I need to find him before Amber does. If she finds him first and convinces him to give her a photo, then she gets my promotion."

"Who's Amber?"

"My nemesis who works at the magazine. She's in town looking for Nolan too and she had a head start."

Damn, there was someone else looking for me? How was I supposed to keep two of them at bay? "So what? You plan on finding him and convincing him to be part of this spread?"

"Short answer, yes, but more than that, I feel like I get him. I wish I could explain it, but his photos, they do something to me. They make me feel something. I want him to know I understand him, and that *Sassy* isn't going to exploit his work. I'm hoping that appeals to him. My job depends on it."

"You do have this way of manifesting what you want. I mean look at you. You always talked about working for a fancy magazine. And now you are."

Her gaze narrowed. "You remember that?"

"Just because you barely noticed me didn't mean I didn't notice you." I pulled into the hotel's parking lot in front of the valet stand. Not giving her a chance to respond, I got out of the car quickly, pulling her luggage out of the trunk and beating the valet to her door to open it. I really needed to stop blurting things out around her.

She accepted my proffered hand. "Thanks, Linc. I have it from here."

Yeah, I should probably just head home, but I was nowhere near ready to say goodnight yet. "If it's just the same, I'll make sure you're settled in? Jilly would have my head if I didn't."

She silently studied me for a minute, then her gaze shifted to my mouth. My heart tripped into full gallop. With our breaths lingering between us in puffs of visible air, my blood hummed just under my skin. But then her gaze shifted away, and the moment was gone.

I led her inside to the lobby and she shifted from foot to foot in her boots. "I don't even have the words to thank you."

"It was just a pickup from the train station. No big deal."

She winced. "Well, that and helping me find Nolan Polk. I owe you."

Cocking my head, I said, "I'll add that to your tab."

At check in, she gave her name and the desk agent searched for it. I took that time to drink in my fill of Nomi. Sure, I would be seeing her a lot over the next couple of days, but I wanted the unfiltered Nomi who didn't have her walls up.

"I'm sorry Miss Adams, but your reservation was cancelled."

Nomi's head snapped up and she glared at the registration attendant. "Please check again. It was booked by *Sassy Magazine*."

"I have, ma'am, and we have one reservation under that booking. A Miss Amber Divine. Your reservation was cancelled. This evening around four."

Nomi shook her head. "That's insane. I was on a flight at that time. You know what, fine. Whatever, just rebook me." She clamped her hands together on the counter; she was the picture of calm, but I could sense the heat coming off her body.

"I'm sorry, we gave the reservation away."

"Excuse me—"

I placed a hand at the small of her back and her jaw snapped shut. Glancing at the attendant's name, I smiled, calling up whatever Porter charm I'd been blessed with. "Karen? I hope you realize the error you've made. Miss Adams is a guest of my family. Senator Porter would be disappointed if you couldn't resolve this problem. There must be something you can do?"

Karen blinked rapidly. "Of-of course Mr. Porter." But after another check through the VIP rooms, nothing was available.

Nomi hung her head. "I'll need to get a hold of Amber and room with her."

"No. You won't. I have another idea. Come with me," I told her.

"Where are we going?"

"Trust me. I know of somewhere better than the Resplendence Inn."

"And you think they'll have rooms days before Christmas?"

"I can guarantee it."

Thirty minutes later, she was standing in the middle of one of the guesthouses on my family's property. "Linc, I don't even know what to say. You're really going above and beyond with this whole white knight thing."

I shoved my hands into my pockets and rocked back on my heels. The smile she gave me was reminiscent of seventeen-year-old Nomi. There was no way I'd crack that shell if she left in a couple of days. I wanted to spend some real time with her. "I know you said you'd owe me."

"Anything. If I have the power to give it to you, it's yours."

Oh boy. My brain decided to conjure up images of her twined around my body naked in front of a fire, and I had to shake my head to get rid of the imagery that would likely drive me insane for weeks. "Go with me to Brad Lennonx's wedding on New Year's Eve?"

Her beautiful mouth fell open. "No way in hell."

I had anticipated that response from her. "How about you sleep on it?"

"My answer's not going to change. Pick something else. *Anything* else."

I considered it. Hell, the way she parted her lips, I considered asking for a kiss instead. But the wedding bought me some more time with her. "Tell you what, we'll talk about it tomorrow."

"Why are you being so stubborn?"

Because I want you. "Because, you never come home and I need a date."

She pursed her lips. "I'll still say no tomorrow."

I casually shrugged. "How about this. If you say yes, I'll finally give you the one thing you've always wanted from me."

5

NOMI

When there was a knock at my door, I assumed it was Linc having forgotten to tell me something, but no, it was Jilly.

When I swung the door open and I saw her bright, wide smile, her inky dark hair piled in a messy bun on top of her head, as well as the bottle of vodka, I grinned. "Hey you."

"Nomi! It's so good to see you." She bounded up to me and enveloped me into a warm hug.

I squeezed her back and let myself settle into the feeling of being home. I missed Jilly. My bestie had been out to LA frequently to see me or we met in places like New York, DC or San Francisco.

"Tell me you have a mixer in here. Linc took you shopping, right?"

I shook my head. "But Instacart is amazing though."

"Excellent. Bring on the cranberry vodka."

I gave her a tight squeeze. "It's good to be home."

"It's good to have you home. To actually hug you again. It's been *ages*."

"Jilly, I saw you three months ago in LA."

"The point is, three months is a very long time without your bestie."

I laughed. "Come on in." I took the vodka from her and brought it into the guest house.

"Oh good, I know Mom had had somebody come and clean it, but it looks cute in here. I haven't been in this one in a while."

"Yeah. Ever since Adam Crooks?"

She gasped and clutched a hand to her heart. "How dare you bring up he who shall not be named?"

I laughed. "Oh my God, remember how you thought you were going to seduce him and no one would have been any the wiser?"

"Yes, but of course he told all his friends, so everybody hung around in the guest house and tried to get a picture. God, guys are such assholes."

"Yeah, but the joke was on them. Because once I saw kids headed onto the property, I promptly told your mother that I was scared and that there were boys creeping around the property. And then your mom and dad had everyone arrested."

She snorted a laugh. "Oh my God that was perfection."

"And then you started the rumor that Adam had a pencil dick."

"Well, he did. In all honesty, I was being truthful."

I laughed and shook my head as I poured us two vodka cranberries and handed her hers. "Oh man we were a menace."

"That we were. How are you? I see you've already gotten settled. You've unpacked I assume?"

I pointed a finger at her. "Don't you judge me for my needing to unpack everything the moment I go somewhere."

"I'm not judging. I think it's very organized and I love it for you."

"Oh Jilly I'm so happy to see you."

We both took our drinks and sat on the tiny couch and she eased back studying me. "You look tired, Nomi."

"Yeah, I do feel tired. It's been a long full day."

"You know that's not what I mean. How are you? I mean, I know work was going well, but you have the look of someone who needs a vacation, a fuck, a steady round of orgasms. Something."

"Oh my God you sound like... I don't know what you sound like."

"I sound like your bestie who loves you."

"Yeah fine whatever. What about you. How are you holding up?"

Jilly squared her shoulders. And I prepared myself for the line of bullshit that would escape. "You know, busy. I'm keeping occupied with the gallery, helping mom with the winery, helping her with dad on occasion. And just trying to get my mind right, therapy's a great thing."

"That I agree on. But how are you really. How are you feeling?"

"When you have your heart broken, everyone always thinks that there's like one path to mending it, you know? But for me I think honestly, I feel okay. Just a little numb. When you have all this time and attention dedicated to someone and then poof they're gone; and you don't know what to do with that extra time, so you just spin in anxiety do you know what I mean?"

"That makes sense. But I heard the word therapy so that's good right?"

She nodded. "Yes. It is good. What I don't love, is everyone treating me with kid gloves still you know? Linc is the worst. I think for him, as my twin, he's the closest to me so he can always feel it, which is terrible because I wouldn't want to put someone through that pain and constant anxiety. That's annoying."

"He's your brother he loves you."

"He's my brother *and* he loves *you*."

A flush crept up my neck. "Would you stop that? He does not *love* me."

"Oh come on Nomi you have to have eyes. Look at him. I think it's gross, but you have to admit my baby brother by a minute, is a hottie. And you know he always had a thing for you right?"

"No he did not. I remember you used to say that and then he would just ignore me or pretend I wasn't there. It wasn't true then it isn't true now."

"Okay, Ms. Denial. When it comes out and he tells you, don't act like you didn't know. Don't do that thing."

"Well, since it'll never happen, I can make that vow easily. I won't pretend I didn't know. I'll be like, 'Oh my God Jilly was right how did I never see it.' Dramatically, I tossed an arm over my forehead and leaned back.

"You always were a drama queen."

"Of course I'm a drama queen but still, he doesn't."

"Like I said, I think it's gross, but you and Linc, I can totally see that as endgame."

"Honey, I'm not having an endgame with anyone."

"Nomi, don't you at least want good sex?"

I blinked at her slowly. "You want me to have good sex with your brother?"

Jilly's face paled. "Again grossness. But, I think that the two of you could be combustible. Unfortunately for me I never ever want to hear about it. I want to see you happy. I want to see him happy. His last fiancé did a number on him."

"He kind of mentioned something about the past being the past, what's that about?"

"She really hurt him. And I could've killed the bitch. I mean I never liked her, but she at least made him happy for a while there. And then she totally used him and broke his heart. I'll never forgive her for that."

My brow furrowed. "In that case I hate her too. And we shall never speak to her again."

Jilly nodded. And for the rest of the night as we sipped on our vodka cranberries and caught up on our lives from the last several months, it felt like home. The fire crackled and the little Christmas tree stood on a stand in the corner. The popcorn was strung together and crossed the high beams of a little cottage. It felt like home. For once in my life, Faith felt like home. But then it always felt like home when I was with Jilly.

It didn't matter where we were, we could have been in a yurt in the middle of the desert somewhere and we still would've made it ours. And that was a way of best friends. As she pushed up to leave, she gathered the glasses and put them in the dishwasher. "Drink some water. I know you are a lightweight these days since all you do is work. I shall see you later okay?"

I nodded. "Oh, actually do you think we can find some time to do a little bit of shopping? I wanted to get Linc a thank you gift for picking me up, being so nice and driving me around town."

She grinned at me. "Sure. But I'm telling you, all you have to do is take off your clothes slap a ribbon up to your titties and call it a day. He would be very happy."

"Oh my God Jilly!"

She scooted out the door and she called out "And whatever you do absolutely positively do not sext him!"

And of course, as I dutifully drank an entire liter of water and got ready for bed, all I could think about was sexting Lincoln Porter.

6

NOMI

The next morning, I tossed and turned in bed. Sexy Linc was *not* part of the bargain. Yes, he could help me and yes, I needed him, but he was not supposed to look like he did. Nor was he supposed to ask me out to the one event I certainly couldn't attend.

And I certainly was not supposed to respond to him like that. Just the thought of his intense, focused, green eyes on me made me feel flushed.

Over the last eight years I had dated some, but nothing serious. After all, my last serious relationship had sent me fleeing my home under the cover of darkness, so I was more than a little gun shy. The guys I dated were nice enough and some with great potential, but I had yet to meet a guy who gave me that same kind of exhilarating rush that my job did. So, I just didn't bother.

The knock on my door came at eight sharp and I was a little surprised to find Linc on the other side. We weren't supposed to meet until eight thirty. "Oh, good morning. I'm almost ready. I just need to finish my make up."

"Sorry I'm early, but I figured maybe we could get breakfast before we head over to Jilly's gallery. Besides, she'd kill me if I didn't bring her a pastry from Claire's bakery."

I smiled. "I see Jilly still has her sweet tooth. How is she doing anyway?" I shoved aside the twinge of guilt. I really didn't want to ask second hand, but Jilly would pretend she was okay for my sake. Her fiancé had called off their wedding in New York just six months ago and she still seemed like she was in recovery mode.

"You know Jilly. She's tough."

"She also puts on a brave face even when she shouldn't."

He gave me that almost smile of his again. The man was dangerous to my equilibrium. "Like someone else I know."

I raised my brow and he pretended not to notice. "You're her twin, so if anyone would know, I suppose it would be you."

"She's still hurt and reeling. But she's good. She's back at work and business is booming. Jilly will bounce back. She always does."

I put down my powder brush. "I was sad to hear about your father. How's he doing?"

Linc shrugged "Fine, I guess. It's hard to see him slipping, you know? Most days he's lucid and he wants to work. But there are days now where he's not even sure of where he is and who people are. It's killing Mom."

"Can't be easy on you either?"

Again, he avoided talking about his father, this time by changing the subject. "After the gallery, do you know where you might want to try next?"

Guilt pricked at me. He had enough things to deal without shuttling me around town. "What about work?"

"I work at the winery for Mom. I'm the Operations Director."

"I'm sure she needs you."

He rolled his eyes. "Everything is shut down until after the holiday. I'm all yours."

The way he said that had sent a tingle through my body and woke nerve endings I hadn't thought about in a very long time.

"I feel bad. I'm sure there are things you'd rather be doing than spending every waking minute with me."

His gaze skimmed over my body. "Not really. How about this? I'll feed you. Take you to see Jilly and we'll see where things go? It probably won't be easy to find this guy, especially if he doesn't want to be found and it is tourist season."

I nodded. "Yeah okay. I just wanted to get this done as quickly as possible so I can get out before the holiday."

He cocked his head. "Not a fan of Christmas?"

"Yeah well, I've been soured on the whole holiday season."

"That's a shame. No eggnog, no caroling, no presents?"

I laughed. "Hold up now. I still like presents. I'm not an idiot."

He nodded, his eyes narrowed imperceptibly. "Lennox really did a number on you."

No. I was not discussing Brad Lennox. "He's not even on my radar. I'm here to work and get out of Faith as fast as my stilettos can carry me. And I'm sorry Linc, but you'll have to think of another way to have me pay you back. I slept on it, and I still can't go to his wedding with you."

His lips tipped up at the corners. "We'll talk about it later. Right now, your taxi service awaits."

I suddenly had a sinking suspicion he wasn't going to let it go. But I was hungry and needed fuel for that kind of fight.

For breakfast he took me somewhere I'd never been, just on the outskirts of Faith. Even though it was still somewhat early, the place was full of tourists, but at least there wasn't a line out the door. If this were LA, there would be at least an hour wait.

While we waited for our food, I studied him. "You know, I realize I don't know you that well. Even back then, I didn't really *know* you, know you. All I know is you run an excellent taxi service and you were sweet enough to offer a girl a lifeline when she needed one."

His laugh transformed his face, making him appear more open, and if possible, more handsome. The sound rolled over me, and made me warm from the inside out, despite the chill outside. "I'm an open book. Ask me anything you want to know."

I widened my eyes. "Anything? You realize as a journalist, my whole job is to ferret out the story I'm looking for right? This is a dangerous proposition for you."

"I think I can take it."

"Don't say I didn't warn you. No evading, Porter. You have to answer honestly."

He shifted in his seat a little, but his gaze never wavered from mine. "Do your worst. Just remember, turnabout is fair play."

I weighed my options. I had no real life to speak of outside of the magazine, so he could ask whatever he wanted. "Fine."

He leaned back to make room for the waitress bringing us our coffee. "Shoot."

I opened my mouth to talk, but decided to take a sip of coffee first. Sighing in contented bliss, I put my cup back down. When I looked at him again, he was staring at me, his green eyes hot and dark.

"What?"

"That look on your face. It's sexy."

I knew I was blushing, but would bet money he couldn't see it. "I see you're starting with the flattery."

"Or truth." He shrugged.

I laughed. This felt like...flirting. *Or maybe you're woefully out of practice.* "You were super smart. I figured you'd go off to law school or something like the rest of the prep school set or bum around Europe. What are you doing back in Faith?"

He opened his mouth, then a light flush stained his cheeks, but he answered. "I did all that. Transferred every AP credit I could and busted my ass to graduate from Carnegie Mellon in three years. Travelled some, came home. Not much to the story."

"Now, why don't I believe you?"

He flashed me another grin. "I did graduate from CMU. Have the diploma to prove it."

"You know what I mean." I said changing tactics. "You could do anything. Go anywhere, be with anyone. Why here?"

"Dad got sick, and the way I figure it, there's plenty of time for me to go do other things. Mom has also needed more help at the winery."

"Are you happy?"

A shadow drifted over his face, but then his good-natured smile was back in place. "Right now, in this moment, yeah. Good food in the company of a beautiful woman."

My heart rate picked up in response. *Easy does it. We're here to work. Not flirt.* For the rest of breakfast, I kept things on safer topics, caught up on some of the people I'd known, local gossip, my job, and our favorite places to travel.

With Linc I could relax and he made it easy to forget where I was, but a flash of red hair outside the window was all the reminder I needed. *Amber.*

She sauntered over with a grin. "I have to admit, Nomi I'm surprised to see you still here. I thought you would have given up and gone back to Los Angeles. I know how much you hate this place."

I forced myself to take a deep breath. "That was Bush league with the hotel Amber."

She blinked wide eyes. "What do you mean Nomi? I didn't do anything to your hotel."

"First, I don't remember giving you permission to call me you Nomi. My name is *Naomi* to you. Secondly, I don't believe you. They cancelled my room after you would have landed and already been here. If you don't have what it takes to beat me on your own, just say that."

She narrowed her gaze. But then it was as if she suddenly realized Linc was sitting there. Her eyes went wide and then her gaze skimmed over him. The broad smile that spread over her lips said she liked what she saw. "Who do we have here? I'm Amber. I work with Nomi. Are you local? Or a tourist and Nomi needed to share your table or something?"

Ew. She was flirting with him. With me right here. And clearly what looks like two people who knew each other having breakfast. God I hated her.

From the flat press of his lips and the slightly furrowed brow Linc wasn't a fan of hers either. But then she didn't know him well. So, as she leaned a hand on the table cocked her hip suggestively with the beaming fuck me smile, she had no idea Linc was about to dismiss her.

"Naomi and I are old friends. You see, I'm allowed to call her Nomi. And no she's right, you did call the Resplendence and cancel her reservation which is juvenile. And before you try to deny it, once I had Nomi me settled at my place, I called to check. My father's a former senator so the Porter name gets you a lot in this place. Front desk clerk was more than happy to spill the beans about how the bossy redhead from Los Angeles insisted the second room was not needed, do you have anything to say for yourself?"

Amber sputtered then. Scrambled for words, and some sort of explanation. But Linc was going in for the kill.

What I loved about him was he was always so calm. He had a deep sense of fairness. And when things weren't fair, he let you know. He probably got that from his dad.

"I swear, she's lying. I didn't mean —"

"You know what I've always hated? People who can't accept responsibility. It's the worst failing of humankind these days.

you would have had a better shot, if you just admitted what you'd done and apologized. But of course, you wouldn't." He turned his attention back to me and gave me a warm smile. "Nomi, darling, I'll meet you at the car."

When he sauntered off, Amber just stared at his back mouth agape. I had to admit I turned to watch the view too because it was magnificent. He stopped at the wooden deep oak hostess stand and paid the bill, before he headed outside, the wind harsh enough to rustle his curls as he stepped into the cold.

Amber scowled behind him. "Who the fuck was that?"

"That was Senator Porter's son, Lincoln. We're old friends."

Amber's mouth hung open. "You could have given me a warning, and he seems like more than a friend."

I shrugged. "Not really your business, is it? If you want to play fair Amber, may the best person win. But what's it like to know that you can't win without going to extreme lengths? The problem is, you miscalculated. I've got a network of friends and support. You're not going to win. And without Lincoln Porter, you're never finding Nolan Polk."

Amber stomped off looking pissed off and determined. I stood then and slid my arms into the coat I'd hung on the back of my chair.

She was going somewhere in a hurry, and I sure didn't have time to sit here on a leisurely breakfast date. I met Linc's gaze with a nod toward Amber. "I see my competition is already up and at 'em. Do you think we can head to Jilly's now?"

He made a poor attempt at hiding his smile. "Sure, car's already warmed up."

I climbed into the passenger seat of the SUV. Maybe if I had been more alert, better mentally prepared, or hadn't wasted part of the morning pretending I was on a breakfast date, I may have noticed the woman coming out of the post office four doors down.

With her smooth chocolate skin and high cheekbones, she was the picture of myself in another twenty years. I froze, not sure what to do. I hadn't called my parents and hadn't planned to. But still, I couldn't ignore the twinge of pain in my heart at seeing my mother again.

Adrenaline spiked through my blood, I knew I had to make a decision. If I didn't move, Mom would see me.

For several loud, pulsing heartbeats, I stayed frozen like that, but then my brain kicked in. Just as my mother was about to look up from her bag, I ducked. I would call home. Just not right now. *Later.* Maybe tonight. Maybe tomorrow. Definitely before I left...*maybe.*

The driver's door swung open and Linc laughed. "What are you doing?"

Sheepish, I sat up. "I, uh, thought I lost an earring."

His brows rose. "Did you find it?"

"Yep," I pointed at my ear. "Put it right back." I could tell that he didn't believe me, but I did not want to get into some long conversation about why I was hiding from my mother.

By the time we reached Jilly's gallery, I felt more at ease. Linc's sister had always been exuberant. It was no wonder she'd been a part of the pep squad at school.

"How did it go earlier, Nomi! Tell me everything. Start talking. Linc helped right? He wasn't annoying?"

"No, Linc was perfect." Damn, why did my voice sound so husky? I cleared my throat. "Did I tell you, I didn't recognize him at first."

Jilly laughed. "That's hilarious. But I guess he's changed a lot huh? Sometimes I can't even believe it. You would think he'd have a girlfriend, but for some strange reason he doesn't. If you ask me, he's carrying a torch for someone."

Linc's brows rose, then he coughed. "Enough, Jilly."

I resisted the urge to shiver while I glanced between brother and sister, and tried to figure out what the sudden note of tension was about. "Jilly, we have so much to catch up on."

My friend squeezed my hand. "We will find a way to make time before you go, okay? In the meantime, I know you didn't come all this way for a snow fix. What do you need? We'll figure it out."

Jilly was someone I could depend on. "So, your gallery has showed some work of one of my favorite photographers."

Jilly nodded, understanding. "Nolan Polk."

"Is there anything you can tell me about him? What he looks like? Any places he might frequent? Even better, where he lives? It's important I get a hold of him."

Jilly bit her lip. "Have you tried his agent? She might know how to reach him best."

I rolled my shoulders. "Yes, repeatedly. I've tried everything. I keep getting the 'Mr. Polk doesn't take unsolicited requests' message. I'm sort of desperate. We're looking to put his photographs in our 20th anniversary issue featuring beauty around the world. I think some of the portraits he's done around the world would be ideal."

"Well, he is extremely talented. No doubt about that. But unfortunately, I can't tell you much about him."

There was something about the way Jilly slid her gaze away when she said that. "Look, I get it. You're protecting your relationship with him. But anything you can tell me would be helpful. What does he like, where might I look next? I'm sort of running out of time."

Jilly slid a glance toward her brother and sighed. "Okay, fine. First place you might look is Faith Woods. He used to do a lot of photos out in the woods. Rumor is he has a cabin there. Then tomorrow night, there's an auction at the country club. Every year for the past three years, he's donated a piece. I doubt he'll be there, but it's worth a shot."

The country club? One of the last places I wanted to go. But if it meant a chance at Nolan Polk, then I had better pull out my little black dress. I turned to Linc, "Looks like we're headed to the woods?"

"You're not Afraid of the woods are you Nomi?"

7

———

LINC

This was insane and I knew it. But, as I quickly learned, there was no deterring Nomi from something she wanted to do. She was too damned stubborn.

"You know, you didn't have to drive me."

I slid her a glance. "Yes, I did." It was the only way to keep her out of trouble. "The roads are a mess out here from the last snow, and you don't actually have a car, so what were you going to do, walk?"

"If it meant getting here ahead of Amber, then yes."

"What is the competition thing with that girl anyway?"

Nomi sighed and wiped away the fog on the passenger side window. "She's hated me since I started at *Sassy*."

I would never understand the dynamics between women. "Girl jealousy bullshit?"

She shrugged. "Something like that. I know I can come off a little strong, but she hated me on sight."

"You? Come off strong?" I teased. That earned me a shove on the shoulder.

"I know I'm driven and that puts people off."

"I dunno. I think it's sexy. You know what you want, and

nothing stands in your way." It also scared the shit out of me, because if anyone could find Nolan Polk, it was *her*. Hell, we were *here*, at *his* cabin.

So stupid. I couldn't risk her knowing who I was just yet. My term with Melanie was up in a little over a week. I had that long to determine if Nomi could be trusted. If she even hung around that long.

I couldn't wait to live my life again without Melanie clouding every decision I made. That was if I even felt like picking up a camera. It had been months since the last photos I took. Though, sitting here with Nomi, with the sunlight streaking in, highlighting the reddish tones in some of her braids, I itched to capture the light and the spun magic in her hair.

Her laugh was low and throaty. "You would be the only man on the face of the earth that finds my relentlessness sexy. Sometimes I feel like I repel guys. It's okay though. I'm about to be the youngest senior editor in the history of the magazine if I can pull this off."

My gut clenched. The way she said it, like it was the thing that would make her whole life, a part of me wanted to give that to her. "I think you're wrong, but it's a moot point. Anyway, we're here."

She sighed. "It's kind of peaceful."

"Don't tell me the city slicker girl is missing her small hometown?"

"Don't get it twisted, I *love* the city. The hustle and bustle. Los Angeles has a way different energy than DC does. But I do like my quiet moments. It must be easy to be creative out here with all this solitude. Nothing to do but listen to your imagination."

It was peaceful. That's why I liked it. I could get away from the noise and just be myself. Granted, I hadn't been here in a while. There was no need.

Nomi opened her door, and a gust of icy wind blew in, chilled me to the bone. Right about now, LA didn't sound so bad, though I had never been. Add in the bonus of Nomi living there, yeah. *Sap.*

I followed her up the front steps of the cabin, her tight ass sashayed in front of me in her leggings. She'd tossed the impractical boots she'd worn yesterday, and opted for flat ones lined with sheep's wool.

Nomi knocked on the door and waited as patiently as she could. After only a brusque knock, she was peering into the windows.

I ignored the twinge of guilt. I knew no one was coming. "Looks like no one is home."

She tsked at me. "Linc, you give up way too easily. Where is your determination?" She hopped down the stairs and started around the back.

"Where are you going? You need to be careful." I could only imagine how pissed she'd be if she slipped on some ice and twisted an ankle.

"I'm fine. I'm not some west coast rube who's never seen snow or ice before."

"Still, been a long time since you've been here, Nomi."

She shrugged. "Last I checked, the stuff doesn't change. Cold, slippery, wet."

"Suit yourself." I couldn't help the smile as she had to check her balance more than once.

At the back of the house, she looked inside the windows again, then frowned. "I don't see anything."

"Nomi, the guy's not home."

"Yeah, but maybe he's fallen down and can't get up and he needs our help. Listen." She stilled and added. "You can almost hear him calling out."

Rolling my eyes I said, "You're ridiculous."

"Surprisingly that is not the first time I've been told that." She scooted around me. "Come on, I need a better view of the whole place."

I stared at her. "You can't break in." Not to my place she couldn't. "Naomi!"

Her laugh rang from around the corner. "Relax, I'm not breaking in. Think of me as more of a peeping Tom."

I joined her at the side of the house and cursed. She was trying to climb a stack of slippery logs to look inside. I stepped up behind her and dragged in a breath of chilly air. *I'm just giving her a lift. No need to get all excited. It's only for a second.* The problem was getting my hands on her was all I could think about.

Nomi looked over her shoulder. "What's the matter? I swear, I only want to have a quick look around. See if there's any indication he's been here or if this is even his cabin."

I knew she wouldn't find anything. I'd paid Hanna, the owner of Faith Woods Cabins, for a cellar to be added. Hell, I even brought in the crew and paid for all the work as a donation so I'd have somewhere to store all his equipment and files. "Fine, let's get this over with."

It wasn't the safest move in the world to touch her since it was all I'd thought about since I picked her up from the train station. I might not be able to stop.

Nomi planted her hands on the sill, and I hoisted her up easily. She might have been tall, but she didn't weigh much. Added bonus, she smelled heavenly. Like chocolate and something else. Something spicier. I had to grit my teeth. All I had to do was not breathe in. "Do you see anything?"

"No," Nomi panted. "Freaking nothing. For a photographer, there isn't a single camera lying around or even a photo. No photography books, no nothing."

"Maybe we have the wrong cabin? Or maybe he was never a

guest here at all." I hated the disappointment in her voice. A snake of guilt slithered over my skin.

"I'm starting to think I'm on a wild goose chase." She sighed. "Okay, coming down."

It would have been an easy task to bring her down slowly. Well, it *should* have been. It would have been no big deal. *Should* have been no big deal. It should have been simple. Key word *should*. But she let go of the windowsill and her shift in weight unsettled us.

Next thing I knew we fell backwards and Nomi gave a little squeak of surprise. I wrapped my arms around her and cradled her inward to protect her body as I landed on my back onto the snow-packed grass. My teeth clinked together as I took the brunt of our fall.

"Oh my God, Linc. Are you okay?"

I did a quick mental check as my tongue ran over my teeth to verify placement. My back had a residual ache I'd likely feel for days. But for the most part, I could feel all my fingers and toes. I was fine. Except....Nomi was now plastered against my body. Her ass nestled right in my lap. I wasn't sure if I was in heaven or hell, either way, my body loved it.

And then the unexpected happened.

8

NOMI

I wanted to melt into the molten heat that surrounded my body, relax into it and nestle there forever. Except, I couldn't. Linc was the source of the heat and right now and I was on his lap.

He sat up abruptly, bringing me with him and I gasped. Through his jeans and my leggings, I felt the insistent pulse of an erection. A very large erection. *Shit*.

Behind me, a wall of muscle braced me upright. In my attempt to scramble up, all I managed to do was rub against him, making my pulse quicken as my breath hitched and heat pooled between my thighs.

Linc planted both hands on my hips, his voice low and gravely as he squeezed gently. "Stop moving, Nomi." He sounded like warm whiskey on a cold night. I instantly stilled.

"W-what?" I could barely force the two brain cells I had left to cooperate enough for speech.

"It'll be easier if you let me pick you up."

Right. "Oh."

Gently, he lifted me and set me next to him on the snow-dusted grass.

Despite the cold of the grass and the whipping air, I felt flushed. Not only did Lincoln Porter have the devil's tempting smile but apparently, he had the power to turn my bones to liquid too.

Just having him hold me on his lap was enough to make my brain conjure all sorts of interesting scenarios about him naked. I cleared my throat in an attempt to dissipate the imagery. What was I supposed to say? *I couldn't help noticing you were working with some serious equipment. Can I help you with that?* No.

I wasn't here looking for a fling. I was here for work. And Linc was doing me a favor. He didn't want me, current erection notwithstanding. I had pretty much given the poor man a lap dance.

Lucky for me, he took all the fumbling words out of my mouth and stood smoothly and extended a gloved hand to me. I swallowed hard, and placed my hand into his. When he spoke, his voice was low. "Tell me Nomi, are you done with your adventures in B&E now?" He pulled me to my feet easily.

"Yeah. It's clear he's not here. If he ever was to begin with."

He watched me with those intense eyes of his and I shifted on my feet under the weight of his scrutiny. "You giving up on me?"

I lifted my chin. "Nope. There's still the auction tomorrow night."

His smile was fleeting. "There's the Nomi we all know and love. Come on, let's head into town."

The drive back to town carried an undercurrent of tension. None from Linc's side apparently, as he chatted with me about happenings in town.

But *I* felt the tension. Every time he touched me. Every time he slanted a grin at me. It was damned inconvenient.

After three more hours searching through the town and a false trail with his post office box, followed by coming up empty handed with Jilly's contact at the bank, I was losing hope. My feet hurt. My back hurt. And to make matters worse, I was still hyper aware of Linc.

He pulled into the guesthouse entrance, and I was surprised to find a car in the driveway. One I recognized. My mother's.

She came out the back entrance before Linc had a chance to even park. Whistling low, he said, "You want me to stay with you?"

I shook my head. I couldn't hide forever. Eventually I'd have to deal with my parents and now seemed as good a time as any. "No, I've got it."

We both climbed out of his car and he headed straight for his room and me for my mother. My mother's no-nonsense stride hadn't changed in the eight years I had been gone.

"Naomi Adams, do you want to explain to me how you come to town and you don't even tell your parents?"

Sighing I answered, "I'm sorry. I was only supposed to be here for a day."

"Naomi." My mother admonished.

I clenched my jaw. I hated that tone. Hated how it made me feel like a misbehaving teenager. Never mind that I'd called my mother weeks ago and had yet to get a call back. But I hadn't come to fight and no doubt Linc and his mother in the main house could hear us. "I'm sorry. I came for work. I should have come by the house. I didn't think it through."

"That's an understatement. Is that why you were hiding from me in the parking lot this morning?"

Damn, she'd seen me. "I wasn't hiding, exactly." I sighed but opted for a little honesty. "I panicked. If I'd had my way I wouldn't have even come back to Faith. And seeing you was sort of a shock to my system."

My mother added more quietly, "When do you leave?"

"I'm not sure actually. I still haven't finished what I came to do."

"Why would you come stay with the Porters when you could have come home?"

What? And have them on my case all the time about how I never came home and how they couldn't possibly make it out to California for some reason or another? My mother had spent her career following Senator Porter around, but, now she claimed she didn't like to travel? "It's a long story. The hotel was over booked and Linc helped me out."

"You could have come home." Mom softened her voice. "Since you're here and the holiday is only a few days away, you should come to dinner, see your father. Christmas Day?"

"I..." The last thing I wanted to do was go home. But I also didn't want to do the same thing I accused them of. "If I'm still here, I'll come."

My mom squared her shoulders. "I know it hasn't been easy. But we haven't seen you in a year and you haven't been home in ages. It will be good for all of us don't you think?"

I thought it just might be torture. But there was no way out. Apparently, coming back to Faith also meant going home. "I'll see, Mom."

"Oh Nomi?"

"Yeah?"

"Will you bring Linc with you?"

9

NOMI

The following night at the auction, after a fruitless day of searching, I was rather tense. After last night's showdown with Mom, it was bound to happen. But when I located the Polk Piece for auction, all the tension rolled out of my body.

It was a beautiful portrait of what looked like northern China or possibly Mongolia. Several children were playing in the snow. Their chubby faces were framed by fur and their wide smiles were the universal kid language of 'this is so fun.' The young girl that he'd focused on, her eyes were a clear, bluish gray. And while she mostly looked like every other child there, she was clearly biracial.

I stared for a long moment before whispering to Linc. "It's gorgeous. You know, I've poured over his work for months and it always takes my breath away. Like he captures the essence of his subject's soul or something."

Next to me, Linc eyed me carefully. "I guess you really like his work?"

I laughed. "Oh come on Linc, you were a photographer once. How can this beauty escape you?"

"It doesn't. Every one of his pieces that I see breaks my heart just a little. I feel like I know that little girl in the photo and her wool covered hands and the joy she feels at playing in the snow." He cleared his throat. "I just like watching your reaction to his work."

"I appreciate beauty. What can I say?" The way he stared at me made me shift from foot to foot. "Let's go find Mr. Polk."

After a dead end with the auctioneer and a peek at the guest list to see who had arrived and checked in, I had to swallow my disappointment. Nolan Polk wasn't here and he wasn't coming. Damn the man was slippery. Almost like he knew I was looking for him and deliberately avoided me.

I left Linc inside greeting guests of the party while I got some air. *Think Naomi, think. If I was a reclusive photographer, where would I hide?* Certainly not Faith, but that was just me.

The one consolation was that Amber hadn't found him either. I had seen her hovering at the edge of the auction talking to one of the guests.

She gestured animatedly to the Polk photo and the man shook his head. Was that her plan? To run around asking any and everyone if they knew him? When she met my gaze, she frowned.

I would never understand what made her hate me so much. Ever since I started at *Sassy*, she'd had me in her crosshairs. and I had to say, this felt like more than general woman competition shit. She acted like I killed her puppy and made her watch.

She sidled up to Linc and offered him a tight smile. he merely lifted a brow at her. She started talked really fast and waved her arms. Then she flapped an arm in my general direction as she pleaded her case.

Whatever their exchange was about, Linc just shrugged and then turned away from her and spoke to someone else. She grabbed for his arm. But something happened, and she lost her balance and pinwheeled. She crashed into one of the waiters with champagne.

The metallic champagne glasses flew everywhere. Luckily, they weren't glass. But, Amber was drenched. I bit the inside of my cheek to keep from laughing and silently thanked the karma gods.

It really shouldn't bother me so much that Amber was here, but I knew the only reason the redhead was doing this was to get under my skin. It wasn't like Amber was a real fan of Polk's work.

"Penny for your thoughts?"

I whirled around to find Linc directly behind me. "Damn it, only ninjas should walk that softly."

He smirked. "What is that they say, walk softly and carry a big—"

I barked out a laugh. "*And* we have a comedian."

He shrugged. "Who said I was joking?"

"That's just it, I know you're not.

\#

LINC

The way Nomi talked about my work, I knew she understood it. *Or you just wanted to believe she understood it.* I wasn't fooling anybody. Least of all myself. I wanted to believe in Nomi because I wanted her. And that was a dangerous mix.

Like Melinda, she was super focused on her job, and getting to Nolan Polk, which was secretly me, was her objective. Once she got what she wanted, she wouldn't be interested in Linc the man, and I at least wanted a shot with her before I told her about my alter ego.

Her smile was slow. "Lincoln Porter, you realize it sounds like you're flirting with me?"

"That's because I am. And it sounds like you're flirting back." The Christmas fairies had also done me a favor. I nodded up at the mistletoe. "You're standing under mistletoe."

She snapped her head up. "Of course I am."

"You know that it is years of bad luck if you avoid a kiss under the mistletoe, right?"

Her laugh was soft, lilting. "It's funny, I hadn't heard that before."

I stepped into her space, and she didn't back away. Instead, she stood her ground and met my gaze. A smile tugged at my lips even as I dipped to kiss her.

The soft brushing of our lips sent a bolt of electricity though my body, and it buzzed at the contact. When she parted her lips on a gasp, I groaned.

I slid a hand up to cup her face, deepened the kiss and angled her head so I could get better access. Her body slowly softened and molded against mine as she reached her hands up to my lapels and drew me closer.

With my body snugly fitted against her, I could think of nothing else but her. She tasted like cinnamon and eggnog and home. Sweet and spicy, her full lips were so soft.

When her tongue slid over mine, I groaned low in my throat and backed her up against the post. My erection kicked against her thigh and Nomi rotated her hips ever so slightly. The motion allowed me to slide a leg between hers, bunching up the skirt of her dress and bringing her heated core in contact with my thigh.

The blood rushed in my head and rational thought escaped me. Her scent swirled around and fogged up my brain. When Nomi's hands slid into my hair, she tugged me closer, helping deepen the kiss.

I slid my free hand from her waist to her ribcage and Nomi gasped into my mouth. With fire in my veins, I traced each of her ribs until my thumb traced the underside of her breast. Her hips rocked into my leg, and I fought the pulsing wave of need that begged me to drag her out of there and get her horizontal.

A crash from behind us had us jumping apart. Heart thudding, I dragged my attention away from her, then back. Her dark eyes were wide with shock and surprise, but need still lingered.

Nomi blinked rapidly, as if trying to bring her brain online, and when she did, she stepped out of my grasp. "*You*, are very dangerous."

I smirked. "I've been dying to do that for eight years, so I had to make it count." The words were out of my mouth before I could stop them.

But it was what she said next that really surprised me. "You should have done that a lot sooner."

"Noted. In that case there are a few other things I intend to do?"

Nomi smirked. "Oh yeah? Like what? Please do go into detail."

This was not part of the plan. With the electricity and need that hummed through my veins, I wasn't complaining, even though my mind reeled. *How had I not known?*

He tugged on my hand gently. "Look, Polk is a no show. I have a surprise for you if you'll come with me."

I slid a glance toward the party. Amber was working the room. Maybe I should too. But for the first time, work wasn't the only thing on my mind.

"Where are you taking me?"

Linc cocked his head. "You're choosing to come with me instead of staying?"

I licked my bottom lip. I could still taste him his woodsy cologne wove an intoxicating web around me. I already had to stay in Faith longer than I thought. I could wait to begin my search in the morning. "Well, when you kiss a girl like that, you leave no room for argument."

His wide grin was enough to stun me into silence. "Come on, I think you'll have fun. And don't worry, I'll help you find Polk. Tomorrow is Christmas, but we'll hit the pavement hard the day after."

I couldn't help my sigh and slid my hand into the warmth of his. "I have to admit, he's more slippery than I thought." *And* the reminder that tomorrow was Christmas made my stomach knot.

"We'll find him." His voice pitched lower. "I'll make sure you get what you're looking for, I promise."

"You shouldn't make promises you can't keep."

He merely winked at me.

"Maybe that will be my Christmas present." I looked up. "You hear that, Santa? I know we don't talk often, but I think I'm due."

Linc's laughter was rich. "Somehow I don't think that's how it works."

"What?" I blinked innocently. "I can't just make demands of Santa Clause?"

"No, but come on, your surprise awaits." His smile turned mischievous, and my breath caught.

Jesus, his smile made my stomach do flips. "What *is* this surprise of yours?"

"I can't tell you. I'll have to show you. If you're up for it?"

If I was— "Is that a dare?"

He shrugged. "Maybe. I mean, you've been living out in Cali with the palm trees and surfer boys. Maybe you've gone soft."

"Soft? Mr. Porter. You should know better than to dare me. Whatever you bring on, I can take."

He nodded as his gaze slid over my body. "In that case, we'd better get you changed."

Thirty minutes later, after a stop back at the house for me to don warmer clothes, we pulled up to the lake and I laughed. "Ice skating? You're kidding right?" Every winter the city cordoned off part of the lake for skating.

He grinned. "What? You're too good to ice-skate? Or is that the fear talking?"

How long had it been since I'd been out on the ice? It felt like a lifetime. Certainly not since I'd left. But when I was younger, it had been a tradition. Every teenager I'd known had been dragged out here for a date or two. It was a popular spot for its fire pits and seclusion. "I'm not scared. You should be though. I used to be quite good."

"Fighting words, I like it."

He pulled a pair of skates out of the trunk and handed them to me. "Jilly said these should fit you. A size 8.5?"

He'd asked Jilly for help? The thought made me flush. Why had I never paid any attention to him before? Maybe if I hadn't been so blinded by Brad, then I would have seen how great he was then.

We laced our skates and he preceded me to the ice, holding out a hand for me. I stared at it dubiously, but Linc merely waited for me patiently. "Trust me. I'll make sure you don't fall." I placed my hand in his. "See. Was that so hard?" he asked.

"No, I guess not. It has been years since I've been ice-skating."

Linc led me around the makeshift rink easily. There were a few other skaters braving the cold. His voice was low when he asked, "Do you miss this place at all?"

I sighed. "When I left, I promised myself I wasn't coming back. I don't think I let myself miss it."

His hand tightened around mine. "Brad was an asshole, but this is your home."

"*Was* my home. I love Los Angeles."

"It seems to suit you."

"It does."

"Did you and your mom work things out?"

I blew a wayward braid out of my face. "Don't remind me. I'm supposed to be there for dinner tomorrow."

"Want me to come with you?"

I gaped at him. "You would do that?"

"Sure, why not? Besides, I like your mom. She was the best chief of staff Dad ever had."

"I've asked enough of you, don't you think?"

He shook his head. "It's no big deal. Besides, my mom will host her Christmas cocktails at ours as usual and I could use a date. We could go to your parents' house after." He was silent for a minute. "You ever going to give me an answer about the wedding?"

I groaned. "Yes, to drinks. It would be nice to see your parents again, especially as they are hosting me. But can't I repay you some other way? I really don't want to go to that wedding."

His voice was soft when he asked, "Do you still have residual feelings for him?"

"No. Hell no. I just don't want to see that crowd again. Zero desire." I slid a glance toward him, and his disappointment was evident. "You really want me as your date?"

"I wouldn't have asked if I didn't."

I couldn't believe what I was about to say, but I did owe him. I even picked up a thank you present for him in town yesterday. And I hoped it would really convey how grateful I was. Because, saying yes didn't seem like enough. "Fine."

"Are you serious?"

"I can't believe it, but yeah, I guess I am. But only for you and Jilly am I staying in this God forsaken town another few days."

Linc picked me up and twirled me around. "Thank you."

"Don't thank me yet. There is a possibility I could still bolt with my hair on fire." Changing the subject, I said, "I remember you used to have pictures in your room of all these places you wanted to travel and see."

He was silent for several minutes. The only sound between us the slicing of our blades on ice. "For a while, I was that guy you know— have passport, will travel. But then things changed."

"Your mom needed you?"

"She did. I mostly help with the winery now. Early on we had to establish a network of support for Dad. That's in place now so she has lots of help."

"But you still stay?"

He shrugged. "It's home, Nomi. And maybe while I'm here, all the noise of the outside world is kept at bay."

"Do you still take photos?"

Linc swallowed hard as he shook his head. "I guess you could say I lost interest."

"That's too bad."

His voice was soft when he said, "I've had other things on my mind."

"That you have." Sliding a glance up at him, I finally asked him the one thing I was dying to since his lips left mine. "So, given that kiss, I take it you're not seeing anyone?"

His grin flashed. "It's a safe bet to say no."

"How come? Clearly you come in some very nice packaging."

A laugh started deep in his belly and rumbled out. "Oh, you think so?"

I flushed. It was way too easy being with him. Felt too good. "Fishing for compliments, Lincoln?"

He plastered a hand to his chest. "Who me?"

"Can't avoid my question." I laughed. "Why no one special for you?"

He raked his teeth over his bottom lip. "There was someone once. It didn't work out."

"Why?"

He sighed. "For starters, we were young. Then, well, she didn't really want me for me. She wanted a piece of me, or rather my name. So that wasn't going to work."

I frowned as I studied him. "I'm sorry. Clearly, it's her loss. She probably regrets taking you for granted."

"I don't know. And I don't care." He twirled me toward the

hot chocolate stand and helped me off the ice. Once we ordered, he asked the same question of me. "What about you? Anyone special since Brad?"

I shook my head. "Nope."

"Oh, come on. You're gorgeous and fun. Add in there, sexy as hell and smart as a whip and most guys I know would be beside themselves trying to get your attention."

I blinked up at him, unsure of what to say, so I took a sip of my hot chocolate to buy some time. The moment the sweet decadent chocolate hit my tongue, I moaned. Linc drew me in for a quick kiss and my heart stuttered. The moment his warm lips brushed over mine like satin, I shivered. He moaned low in his throat and made me want to lean in.

When he pulled back, I couldn't help my whimper of disappointment. "Sorry. I've been thinking about doing that since we left the party."

I blinked up at him even as I struggled to find the words. "You have a way of surprising a girl."

He laughed. "You can't be surprised that I'm attracted to you."

"It's not that; you just never seemed to pay me much attention back in high school."

He kissed me again softly and he tasted like hot chocolate. "Oh, I noticed you. You just weren't paying attention to *me*. And you were with my best friend. I was wrong to want you. I spent a lot of time staring at you though. Whenever you came to the house to hang with Jilly, it was the sweetest torture in the world. I had all these elaborate scenarios in my head of how you'd kick Brad to the curb and go out with me."

What? "How come you never said anything?"

"You were with Brad. It was like you didn't see anyone else. Besides," He shrugged. "You were out of my league. I was also an idiot and thought Brad was my friend."

He had to be kidding. "I obviously made a mistake with Brad then. I have a habit of not picking the best guys. When I started at our school, he sort of swooped in and just took over. Like I was an inevitability. I always hated that. But I don't think I was smart enough to really see him for what he was back then."

"An asshole."

I laughed. "I see there's no love lost."

Linc rolled his shoulders. "He was a dick, poked at me whenever he could. He only wanted me to be his friend because of Dad. I think it secretly chapped his ass that I was well liked."

I rolled my eyes. "I know I was heartbroken at the time, but I dodged a bullet."

"Yeah, you did."

"So, if you don't really like him, then what are you doing going to his wedding?" I asked.

Linc's lips pressed flat momentarily. "I'm standing in for Dad. He was invited. Well, he and my mother really. Since Mom has been looking after my father, she doesn't really do the social things that used to be an integral part of her schedule."

"That's understandable."

He shrugged. "Jilly and I stand in for them usually."

"Why aren't you taking Jilly to the wedding then?"

His smile was slow and dangerous. "Because I would rather be going with you."

"Are you sure this is going to be okay?"

11

NOMI

At the end of the night, I paused at the door, unsure of where this was going to end. Unsure of where I wanted it to end. "Thank you for tonight. For all of today and yesterday really. It was fun. I don't think I've stopped to relax in a long time."

Linc's smile was lopsided. "Happy to be of service. Next time we race around the rink, be warned, I'm not letting you win."

The laugh bubbled out of me before I even registered it. "You sound like a sore loser, Linc." Tonight was the most fun I'd had in a long time. For once, I didn't think about work first. He'd even managed to tease me into a race. I still wasn't sure if he'd let me win or not, but I was going to take gloating rights where I could get them.

His smirk morphed into a mock look of shock. "How am I supposed to sound? I thought you were out of practice. How was I supposed to know I was dealing with a ringer?"

I giggled. "Don't be salty. If you're good, I'll give you a rematch."

He perked up then, standing a little straighter. "You're on."

"Hell, I'll even give you a slight handicap."

His laugh was deep and rumbling and it made the hairs on my arms stand up. I liked being with him, more than I should.

"Nomi?" He took a step into my space and his voice dropped an octave.

"Yeah, Linc?"

"Since you cheated, I'm claiming my reward."

My hackles rose at the statement, but the desperate need to feel his hands on my body overrode my competitive nature with a deep pulling lust. I nervously licked my lips and met his gaze. "What do you want your reward to be?" Electric sparks danced over my skin.

"A kiss," He whispered. His moss green eyes darkened to nearly black and I held my breath. His gaze dipped to my lips as he wound his hands around my waist.

Before I could even blink, he pressed his lips to mine. The kiss was firm and coaxing to begin, but an unseen match lit my body on fire. My lips parted on a surprise gasp and Linc took advantage. His tongue dipped in and coaxed mine into a dance.

I instinctively wound my arms around his neck, tentatively twining my fingers into the hair at the nape of his neck. When the pads of my fingers made contact with his skin, he growled and pressed me closer against him. Through his jeans, his erection nudged at my cleft, and I arched my body into his, needing to feel more of him, needing to be closer. For once, for this moment in time, I would give in to it.

But then Linc did the one thing I didn't expect.

***

LINC

I dragged my lips from hers, dragging in deep shuddering breaths. It was my feeble attempt at trying to gain some control over the situation.

Nomi tasted so good. Sweet, with just a hint of a spicy bite.

The need roiled inside me, making me shake. I'd wanted to touch her for so long and now that I had, my senses were in overdrive. I drew back, and tried desperately to pull oxygen into my lungs.

She made a tiny mewling sound in the back of her throat before her eyelids fluttered open. Her dark eyes were obsidian now, heavy with lust. Her full lips parted. Perfect for kissing.

She ducked her head and shook it slightly.

I lifted her chin so she had to meet my gaze. "What's the matter?"

"I'm not staying, Linc."

My heart pinched. But I wasn't a fool. I would rather have her with me for a few days, than not at all. "C'mon Nomi, take a chance."

We stood outside her door, looked in each other's eyes for seconds, minutes, hours. Finally, she raised up on her tiptoes and looped her arms around my neck. "Maybe it's time to welcome me home."

Her lips were feather light and cotton candy soft as she brushed against my own. I let her lead the slow fusion of our lips, allowing her to be in control, despite how much I wanted to take charge. To push her to open for me. Push her to *see* me. To see how I felt about her. But I forced my body under control. Forced my mind behind the reigns and not the thick, sweet, thrumming of desire.

Nomi released one hand to fumble with the door behind her. I helped her out and took the key and the lock and walked us inside and slammed the door behind us.

I pulled her against me, molded her body to mine. My erection throbbed against her belly and blood rushed in my ears as I dipped my tongue in her mouth.

Nomi drew in a shuddering breath, and I groaned, the little breathy sounds she made drove me crazy. I turned us around to brace her against the door and she moaned and tilted her hips into my body.

Skin on fire, I tore my lips from hers to kiss along her jaw. Nomi whimpered while she tried to drag me closer. When I reached the hollow of her neck, right behind her ear, I sucked gently, relishing in the shiver that wracked her body.

"Linc..."

I wanted to consume her. Lust made my head swim. I needed to get my shit under control, or I was going to lose it.

But Nomi didn't help. She slid her hands under my coat, then tugged up my sweater. The moment her hands slid over my lower back, my skin flamed.

I hitched her up, planting myself more firmly between her legs, and she wrapped those long stems around my waist. The result was my cock nudging against her sweet, heated cleft. "You are so perfect."

She moaned, my name and I nipped at her neck. "Tell me, Nomi. What do you like?"

12

NOMI

I moaned. From my toes to my thighs, my breasts to the roots of my hair; my whole body was on fire for Linc. He rocked his body into mine again and I whimpered. The way he nudged me with his steel length, I was already strung tight, too tight, ready to snap.

With an impatient snarl, he tugged my jacket free, and there was a tangle of arms and contortions to get it off. He yanked off his own more easily, all while I was bracketed against the door by his hips.

His hands stole under my Henley, and he hissed as he nuzzled my neck. "So soft." He mumbled.

My head spun as I tried to make sense of what he made me feel, but the thrumming desire in my blood eventually just took over. When he went back to kissing me, he held my face in his hands, expertly slanted his lips over mine and took over and commanded the kiss. He slid his tongue over mine, sipped and sucked on it, until my mind fogged and all I could think about was how to get closer to him. Melding our bodies and never letting go.

I tugged on his sweater, and I could feel him smile into the kiss as he dragged it up. He broke our contact to release it over his head. I slid a glance over his pectorals, then his abs.

The smug smile was even in his tone as he said, "My turn." He tugged my Henley up hem first and pulled it over my head. Too weak to make my arms work properly, I just let him do the work. The shirt made the same soft thud his had.

Linc's eyes locked on my breasts and watched in fascination as I took a deep breath.

He never took his gaze off of me as he smoothed his hands up over my ribs. I sucked on my bottom lip as his hands drew closer to my breasts.

When Linc reached my bra, he paused and dragged his gaze up to my eyes. He waited until he had my full focused attention before dragging his thumbs over the lace covering my nipples.

Unable to look away, the tension coiled inside me snapped. The fast hard orgasm spiked through me like a lighting bolt. With electric sensations lighting me up internally like a Christmas tree, I rolled my head back and broke eye contact.

"No, baby look at me. I want to see what you look like when you come."

I dragged leaden eyelids up to meet his burning gaze. Even as an aftershock skipped through my body and made me weak, he watched with a focused intensity. He looked like a man ready to feast.

Sexy and low, his voice tripped over my skin like a caress. "Do you have any idea how beautiful you are?"

Slowly he rolled my nipples between his thumb and forefinger through the fabric. The motion sent a spike of lust through me, straight to my core. "I could watch you respond to my touch all day."

I wanted him to do more than watch. I wanted him closer, his body over mine. Inside as he filled me and made me slow down and see only him.

Linc lifted me away from the door and carried me to the bedroom. He lowered my feet to the floor and kissed me leisurely, like we had all the time in the world.

He took his time even though I could feel how hard he was, how much he wanted me. With one hand, he unfastened my bra and helped me slide my arms free.

The back of my knees hit the bed and I reached for his belt. But he stayed me with a hand. Leisurely kissing me, he removed his belt himself, shucked his jeans off and tossed something onto the side table.

Wallet maybe? He never once broke our kiss. With his boxers still on, he lay me down on the bed, followed me down and nestled between my thighs. He kissed me slowly, explored the depths of my mouth and took his time. His hands were playful as they skimmed my body.

Now that my breasts were free, he all but ignored them. He teased and kissed the valley between and brushed his lips along the undersides, but the only contact he made with my nipples was to blow over the peaks lightly.

When I attempted to drag him closer to my breasts, he lightly palmed one before wrapping his lips over the sensitive bud and licked leisurely.

"Oh God, yes," I moaned and clutched his head to me.

He teased me with his teeth and I arched my body into the caress, pulling him close. He slid his hand down my torso, over my stomach to the elastic edge of my leggings. My breath hitched and my hips rose, instinctively seeking his touch.

He took a slow pulling tug at my breast and teased the tip. All the while, he slid his hand under the elastic. His fingers were like heat seeking missiles. When he found my slick center, he moaned against my skin. "Fuck, you're wet."

He slid a long finger inside of me and I rocked my hips into him, begging for more. I needed him deeper. "More."

When he slipped another inch into me, I cried out. He kept a steady rhythm, sinking into me as he kissed his way down my chest. Only pausing long enough to yank my leggings down my legs.

When I lay bare before him, Linc kissed his way up my body and splayed my legs wide. With one deep stroke of his tongue, I shook and clawed at the pillows behind me, afraid to let go lest I break into a million pieces. As he traced circles around my clit, he stroked me deep with his fingers, drew out slowly, let me feel every inch of his strokes and made me crave more of it. Made me need it.

He suctioned his lips over my hypersensitive clit, and I shook violently. He sucked deep again, made me break apart in his arms. With what sounded like a grunt of satisfaction, he kissed my inner thighs, pulled himself up my body and kissed me lazily and strategically and made my blood spike again.

Still, he avoided my breasts. Instead, he chose to kiss up my sternum, my clavicle, and then nuzzled my neck. When he reached my lips, he kissed me deep and I could taste myself on them. His fingers sank into my hair. And all that stood between our bodies was the thin layer of his cotton boxer briefs.

He fisted my hair, tugged a little and made me arch my neck for him. All the while, he rocked his hips against me. The full length of his erection pulsed against my clit.

"Fuck. I want to sink into you so bad. Do you have any idea how many times I fantasized about this? Do you know how many times I would dream about you in the shower? Do you know how many times I had to wrap my fist around my cock and stroke myself just to get a little relief from you?"

"Oh my God, Linc." Every dirty word whispered against my skin was like an aphrodisiac. I needed more. I *wanted* more.

He used his teeth against the skin on my neck, lightly grazed, then nipped. And sucked hard. "I wondered about you so many times. I wanted to know what you were doing, who you let touch you."

Beneath him, I rocked my hips upward. Desperate for him to slide all the way home, but his stupid boxers were in the way. "Linc, please, I need you."

"I have needed you for years. Years, Naomi. That's a long time to need someone. Do you have any idea what it's like? To want someone so bad you know you can't have. Everything they do makes you hard. But it wasn't just that I wanted you. I wanted your laughs. I wanted your smiles. I wanted you to share everything with me."

His kisses were more gentle now. But his hips we're working me with a slow grind. I lifted and rotated my hips, silently begged him to do something about his boxers. He eased one hand out of my hair, and brought it down to cup my face as he kissed me. And he continued to slid his hand down to cup my breasts. When he started rolling my nipple gently again with his thumb I shuddered. The orgasm started to climb and climb and I just wanted release.

"But all that time, it was like you were teasing me. I knew you weren't. It didn't stop me from needing you. As I got older I thought of you, and wondered what you were like. What foods caused that little moan at the back of your throat. What made you laugh, what made you cry."

How was he doing this? He didn't just seduce my body. Though his thumb that rolled my nipple and his massive erection that ground against my clit we're doing a damn good job. He told me how much he'd wanted me. All the ways he'd wanted me. He let me know he'd seen me, the real me.

"You've lived in my fantasies as long as I've known you. I did wonder how your mouth would look wrapped around my cock. If you'd let me fuck you raw, if you'd let me put a baby inside you, if you'd let me play with your ass."

The next orgasm ripped through me making the arch my back and whimper as my head thrashed back and forth on my satin pillowcase.

His little chuckle was the sexiest thing I'd ever heard.

"Oh my God, holy shit"

He chuckled into my hair. "That's a good girl," He whispered as he eased back. when he stood reaching for his wallet on the side table, I lazily sat up and followed him.

I reached for his boxers, teased my fingertips against the elastic and made him freeze and his body go rigid. "Naomi," he growled. The guttural tone made me even wetter.

I blinked up at him and whispered, "Yeah."

"I—uh..." When I reached inside his boxers and palmed his throbbing erection, he stopped being coherent.

I hesitated too. Holy shit he was huge. My gaze was transfixed by the bulge in his boxers. "Wow. This is uh..." What Was there really to say? The man was carrying around a proverbial lead pipe in his trousers. Thick and long.

"You keep staring at him like that and this will be over before we even—" his voice cut off when I gave him a little squeeze.

"Were you saying something, Linc?"

His head fell back as he shook it. "N-no. Fuck no."

I eased his boxers down and swallowed hard when I came face to face with the thick length of him.

Christ, he was enormous. Nine inches at least, and I might have to use two hands here.

Don't be a coward.

I wanted him. I wanted *this*. And if I was being honest with myself, there was a part of me that had noticed him watching me back then. But maybe I'd felt like I'd made my bed with Brad, and I wasn't going to be that girl that went from one friend to the other. So, I'd shoved away any residual feelings about him.

But now that he was here, right in front of me, I salivated.

I stroked the length of him, teasing the crown with my thumb, ran it over the soft, smooth tip. "That's what I thought."

Gently, I retreated to the base and back again with both hands. As he hissed, Linc sank his hands into my hair again. I circled the crown of his erection again with my thumb and one of his hands snapped to my wrist. "Nomi— Do you have any idea how close I am right now?"

I sucked on my bottom lip as my gaze dipped to his impressive erection. "You can show me."

With a growl, he gathered both of my hands in his and pushed me back down onto the bed. His big body loomed over mine. I assumed he stepped out of his boxers. As he lay over me, he locked my hands into the handcuffs of one of his. "You are a naughty girl."

His cock, now free, pulsed insistently at the apex of my thighs. He notched his hips forward and the tip grazed my opening. I threw my head back. "Oh my God, Linc."

Clearly, a glutton for punishment, since I couldn't use my hands. I raised my hips ever so slightly, and encouraged the contact again.

He cursed low. And notched the blunt head of his cock just inside my opening. "Fuuuck me, Nomi. Damn you feel incredible."

I wanted more. Even though just part of the tip was enough to stretch me. I couldn't help gently trying to suck him in; the little pulsing motion as automatic as breathing.

"Fuck. Fuck. Fuck," His whole body shook above me now. He retreated and pulled his hips back. And then with a groan he notched forward again. This time he sunk into me just a little bit more.

My eyes flared open against the tight fit. "Linc? Oh God."

He gritted his teeth and dropped his forehead to mine. The hand clamping my wrists together squeezed them gently. "Shhh baby. I know. I'm too big. I'm sorry." He tried to pull back, and in a panic, I wrapped my legs around him driving him even further forward.

We both hissed. He was so big. Dear God.

"Fuck. You naughty girl," He nipped my ear lobe. "If I don't go slow, this is going to hurt."

I nodded. As if I understood. but he was trying to take away my new favorite toy. he eased back and I whimpered. But then he was back. With just the tip, he shallowly penetrated me and drove me mad. "Damn it, Lincoln, stop teasing me and make love to me."

He brushed his lips against mine again. "I'm sorry, this just feels so good." He gave my hands another gentle squeeze. "Can you be a good girl and keep them here or will you be your usual stubborn and obstinate self?"

I giggled. "I can play nice. For now."

He laughed and shook his head as, he rolled away and pulled a condom out of his wallet sheathed himself. When he rolled back and settled between my thighs, his expression was of mock surprise. "Will wonders never cease? You listened to me."

I shrugged, "It's been known to happen."

He nipped my shoulder. "Cheeky." As he placed hot, open-mouthed kisses along my neck and jawline, he teased one of my nipples into a hardened bud with his fingers. Desire spiked in my blood, and I bit my lip as I angled my hips up.

On first contact, Linc cursed. I blinked up innocently. "Look, Linc, no hands."

He laughed and sucked my bottom lip into his mouth. "*You* are a rule breaker."

"Bender. I'm a rule *bender*."

I lifted my hips again and Linc held me in place. "Nomi, I'm trying to slow down."

I shook my head. "We can go slow next time. I need you

now." I emphasized my desperation with another slow roll of my hips.

"Hell." Linc dropped his forehead to mine as he pressed into me. He shifted both hands to mine, interlacing our fingers as he slid into me. Despite my need, he took his time. Sweat popped on his brow as he rocked into me. Slow slide, then even slower retreat. Deeper slide, another retreat. He played me like a violin, built my desire like a crescendo.

Patience had never been one of my virtues, so I had to break one of his rules. I freed one hand, wound it around his back and scored the flesh lightly with my nails. Linc's breath hitched, and his hips increased their tempo just a little bit.

But I wanted more. I wanted him to lose control, just like I was, wanted him to possess me. "I won't break, Linc, make love to me. Please." I punctuated my plea with another taste of my nails.

His answering growl was low as he scooped a hand under my ass and tucked me closer against him. Control gone, he gave me what I wanted, marked me with love bites, and dragged me to the peak of the mountain.

Linc reached between us, found the little bundle of nerves that was the key to my pleasure, pressed on the button gently, and as he sank deep, he whispered against my lips. "Come for me, Nomi."

And I did, I broke apart in his arms as he loved me. As a starburst of bliss cascaded through my body, he tensed above me and held me tight to him.

"Are you on the pill Nomi?"

I dragged my heavy eye lids open and nodded.

Even as he rocked his hips, he growled. "Good. One day, I'm going to fuck you raw."

13

NOMI

I turned towards the wash of sunlight and stretched my arms over my head. My body ached in places I'd long forgotten about. The beard burn on my breasts, the deep ache between my thighs, the rug burn on my back from the middle of the night session with Linc reminded me that I had never had that much fun in my entire life. My knees still ached from when I'd wrapped my mouth around the thick length of him in the shower.

Linc.

I snuggled deeper in the bed. I'd really slept with Linc. And not just slept with him, but had sheet clawing, body aching, sex so good B.O.B. would never do again. That man knew his way around my body.

I cracked an eye open to glance at the clock. 7 AM. That meant it was officially Christmas morning. With a groan I rolled over, only to roll into a wall of muscle.

Linc's voice was deep and raspy. "Do you know you sleep like a crazy person? I woke up twice to keep you from rolling off the bed. I was worried you'd hit your head or something."

My eyes popped open and I scrambled back in bed several inches. "Linc," I gasped.

His grin was slow and sexy. "I'm glad you remember my name. I don't think I heard it enough last night." He licked his bottom lip then whispered, "Come here."

"I-uh, what are you doing here?"

He raised an eyebrow. "Well, if you let me, I'd like to taste you again."

A warm flush started in my chest, then crept over my body. "I mean, I thought you would have left."

His brows snapped down. "Did you want me to leave?

I shook my head quickly. "N-No. Of course not. I didn't know if you were staying and after the last time, I sort of passed out."

Linc shook his head even as he pulled me to his warm body. "Nowhere else I'd rather be this morning."

I searched my brain, but all I could come up with was, "Oh."

"Relax, Nomi, and let me hold you."

I didn't need to be told twice. As soon as I was encased in his strong hold, my body started to melt. "Sorry. I just didn't expect you to stay."

"I gathered."

How was I supposed to tell him that when I slept with someone the tacit agreement was that they were gone in the morning? "I hope I didn't keep you up."

His laugh was quick. "Are you kidding? After the thing you did with your tongue, I think I was in a coma."

I tucked my head and laughed into his chest. "Okay truth be told, I *was* a little worried I'd killed you."

"And what a way to go." He kissed my forehead, then sat up. "I have something for you."

I blinked. "Oh wow, you didn't have to get me anything. Especially after you've been so nice and shuttled me around."

He pushed the covers back and stood. My mouth went dry

at the sight of his strong powerful body. Linc was all lean muscle, tanned, smooth skin, and powerful, but somehow graceful. He moved like a man who was comfortable in his own skin.

He rummaged in the bag he'd brought with him skating last night. When he turned around, he was semi erect, and it gave me a couple of sinful ideas.

His gaze turned hot when he tracked the direction of my gaze. With a smirk he said, "Keep looking at me like that and we're not getting out of bed this morning."

Right about now, not getting out of bed sounded like a fantastic idea. *Don't go getting all attached girl, you're not staying. You have a life in Los Angeles. Do. Not. Get. Attached.* Only problem was, I liked him. And I liked how he made me feel. Slightly on edge, like anything could happen. "Who said anything about getting out of bed?"

His smile was quick as he climbed back into bed with me. "But first I want to give you this before you put another spell on me and actually do put me in a coma this time."

I sat up and eyed the small box he held in his hands. I did love presents. "You know you shouldn't have."

He eyed my chest. "How about you drop your sheet, and we'll call it even?" He winked.

"You're easy aren't you?"

"Yep."

I shook my head. "You're going to have to work a little harder than that."

His grin turned wolfish. "Done." He held out the box to me.

Sitting there, bare chested, with the sheet thrown over his lap, holding out a present to me, he looked a little like how I remembered him. Boyish and silently watchful.

I accepted the box and studied it carefully. "Is shaking allowed?"

His eyes widened. "Why would you want to? Aren't you just going to rip it open?"

I made a face of mock alarm with wide eyes and formed an 'O' with my mouth. "What? Half the fun is guessing."

The corners of his lips tipped into a smile. "Then by all means, shake. Gently."

"Too small for shoes."

He shook his head. "No. Not shoes."

I made a series of guesses, each more outrageous than the last. And he laughed along with me. Finally, I just gave in and tore the paper open. When I lifted the cover of the plain pink box my breath caught. Nestled inside was a music box with a ballerina on top.

My heart thundered, and all of a sudden there wasn't enough air. I couldn't breathe.

When I didn't say anything, just stared at the music box, Linc filled the silence. "I hope I got it right. I remember that you used to really like them."

My hands shook as I reached out to finger the delicate ballerina on top. "It's beautiful." I glanced up at his expectant face. "I don't know what to say. When did you get this?"

"Yesterday when you and Jilly were chatting. Did I get it right? I remember when you were kids, Jilly got you one for Christmas once. I also remember you used to dance, so I figured maybe a ballerina or something. If you don't like it, I can return it."

I snatched up the box and held it to my chest. "No. I mean it's too much, and you shouldn't have gotten something so extravagant."

He just shrugged. "I know how hard it is for you to come home. I wanted to give you something special so you'd remember it well."

Oh hell. Tears pricked my eyelids and I blinked them back

rapidly. I was not going to cry. Despite myself, tears welled in my eyes, "I don't know what to say."

"Say you love it."

I grinned broadly before launching myself into his lap and wrapping my free arm around him. "I love it. Thank you. You've been great, and I know I was a bit of a pain in the ass the last couple of days and I'm sorry. I am really grateful to you." I sat back, the box still clutched to my chest. "Which is why I'm so glad I did a bit of shopping the other day for you."

His brows shot up. "When? And I didn't expect—"

I waved him off with a hand. "It's not anything big. But I asked Jilly what would be a nice way to say thank you. She made what I hope was a good suggestion."

"Still, you didn't have to, Nomi. I was happy to help. Besides, it gave me some time to hang out with you. Which is all I really wanted anyway."

"Would you shut up and just open it? If possible, I love giving presents more than I love getting them." I pulled a box from the bedside drawer and handed to him.

Linc stared at the box for a moment, then up at me. "Thank you, Nomi."

"No, honestly, thank you. You've been great and well, I figure I should repay your kindness for agreeing to go with me to my parents' house tonight."

"Don't forget you're already going to drinks with me at my folks' house, so this really wasn't necessary."

"Okay, fine, then look at it as a helping me love Christmas again present. I don't know. Just open it."

I bit my thumbnail nervously. Maybe I'd been too presump-tuous. Maybe he wouldn't want it.

He lifted the lid off the box and his body went still. For several long moments thick silence hung in the chasm of space between us.

Unable to take it for much longer, I started to ramble. "I'm sorry if it's not what you would have wanted. You said you didn't do that anymore. But I remember you being really good, so I thought maybe it was a time thing. Maybe I could remind you how much you loved it like you reminded me last night that there are some things about being here I love. Is this okay?"

Linc held up the 50mm camera and examined it. Silently, he removed the lens cap, adjusted the lens, then snapped a photo of me.

Oh shit. I ducked. "Oh my God, Linc! What are you doing? I don't have any make up on and I'm pretty sure I'm raccoon eyed from last night. And *hello*, naked here."

He laughed. "You look beautiful. Besides, that sheet is covering more than your dress did last night."

I clutched the sheet closer to myself and put out my hand to keep him from taking any more photos. "You're nuts."

He laughed. "Maybe, but I'm also extremely grateful. It's been a while since I held a camera. I guess I've been looking for a reason to love it again."

"I know it's not fancy. Hell, it's not even digital, but maybe you can play around with it a little." She shrugged. "I don't know." I was unused to feeling unsure.

He tucked a finger under my chin. "It's perfect. Thank you."

"You're welcome."

"Now are you sure you won't let me shoot some pictures of you? I'm feeling inspired."

I laughed. "Absolutely not."

"Fair enough, then how about I thank you properly." He gently placed the camera on the bedside table and took the box from me.

"Lincoln Porter, you look like you have something no good planned for me."

"Oh, I think you'll like it."

I giggled. "You know what they say, talk is cheap."

He moved so swiftly, he surprised me; before I knew what was happening, he had me on my back and had worked his way under the sheet between my thighs. He kissed my inner thighs lightly and I squirmed.

He blew gently over my sex, and I slid my fingers into his hair, relishing in the luxuriant feel of it.

"Do you have any idea how good you taste?" To demonstrate, he lapped at me and moaned as though he was starved for me.

I clutched for purchase on the sheets even as I held his head in place and rotated my hips into his questing mouth.

Linc varied his strokes, brought me to the edge, then drew back, teased, soothed, and quieted the fever. When he felt the desperate tension ebb out of my body, he ratcheted the tension back up again, slid his tongue as deep as it would go inside of me and drew breathy, desperate cries from me.

The orgasm started in my spine, slowly rolled out, and hit every nerve, every cell, and every corner of my soul.

With a growl, he splayed me wide with strong hands and didn't relent; he applied the pressure just how I liked it. Even as I shook and my body shivered, he didn't yield. He continued to lick and stroke me. Linc pulled a response from me, marked me as his. He never let me forget what he could do to my body.

It was only after he dragged another sobbing release from me that he kissed my thighs gently as he moved up my body. He tucked my limp body against his as he nuzzled my neck. "Get some rest Nomi. You're going to need it. I have some big plans for you today."

I turned towards the wash of sunlight and stretched my arms over my head. My body ached in places I'd long forgotten about. The beard burn on my breasts, the deep ache between my thighs, the rug burn on my back from the middle of the night session with Linc reminded me that I had never had that much fun in my entire life. My knees still ached from when I'd wrapped my mouth around the thick length of him in the shower.

Linc.

I snuggled deeper in the bed. I'd really slept with Linc. And not just slept with him, but had sheet clawing, body aching, sex so good B.O.B. would never do again. That man knew his way around my body.

I cracked an eye open to glance at the clock. 7 AM. That meant it was officially Christmas morning. With a groan I rolled over, only to roll into a wall of muscle.

Linc's voice was deep and raspy. "Do you know you sleep like a crazy person? I woke up twice to keep you from rolling off the bed. I was worried you'd hit your head or something."

My eyes popped open and I scrambled back in bed several inches. "Linc," I gasped.

His grin was slow and sexy. "I'm glad you remember my name. I don't think I heard it enough last night." He licked his bottom lip then whispered, "Come here."

"I-uh, what are you doing here?"

He raised an eyebrow. "Well, if you let me, I'd like to taste you again."

A warm flush started in my chest, then crept over my body. "I mean, I thought you would have left."

His brows snapped down. "Did you want me to leave?

I shook my head quickly. "N-No. Of course not. I didn't know if you were staying and after the last time, I sort of passed out."

Linc shook his head even as he pulled me to his warm body. "Nowhere else I'd rather be this morning."

I searched my brain, but all I could come up with was, "Oh."

"Relax, Nomi, and let me hold you."

I didn't need to be told twice. As soon as I was encased in his strong hold, my body started to melt. "Sorry. I just didn't expect you to stay."

"I gathered."

How was I supposed to tell him that when I slept with someone the tacit agreement was that they were gone in the morning? "I hope I didn't keep you up."

His laugh was quick. "Are you kidding? After the thing you did with your tongue, I think I was in a coma."

I tucked my head and laughed into his chest. "Okay truth be told, I *was* a little worried I'd killed you."

"And what a way to go." He kissed my forehead, then sat up. "I have something for you."

I blinked. "Oh wow, you didn't have to get me anything. Especially after you've been so nice and shuttled me around."

He pushed the covers back and stood. My mouth went dry at the sight of his strong powerful body. Linc was all lean muscle, tanned, smooth skin, and powerful, but somehow graceful. He moved like a man who was comfortable in his own skin.

He rummaged in the bag he'd brought with him skating last night. When he turned around, he was semi erect, and it gave me a couple of sinful ideas.

His gaze turned hot when he tracked the direction of my gaze. With a smirk he said, "Keep looking at me like that and we're not getting out of bed this morning."

Right about now, not getting out of bed sounded like a fantastic idea. *Don't go getting all attached girl, you're not staying. You have a life in Los Angeles. Do. Not. Get. Attached.* Only problem was, I liked him. And I liked how he made me feel. Slightly on edge, like anything could happen. "Who said anything about getting out of bed?"

His smile was quick as he climbed back into bed with me.

"But first I want to give you this before you put another spell on me and actually do put me in a coma this time."

I sat up and eyed the small box he held in his hands. I did love presents. "You know you shouldn't have."

He eyed my chest. "How about you drop your sheet, and we'll call it even?" He winked.

"You're easy aren't you?"

"Yep."

I shook my head. "You're going to have to work a little harder than that."

His grin turned wolfish. "Done." He held out the box to me.

Sitting there, bare chested, with the sheet thrown over his lap, holding out a present to me, he looked a little like how I remembered him. Boyish and silently watchful.

I accepted the box and studied it carefully. "Is shaking allowed?"

His eyes widened. "Why would you want to? Aren't you just going to rip it open?"

I made a face of mock alarm with wide eyes and formed an 'O' with my mouth. "What? Half the fun is guessing."

The corners of his lips tipped into a smile. "Then by all means, shake. Gently."

"Too small for shoes."

He shook his head. "No. Not shoes."

I made a series of guesses, each more outrageous than the last. And he laughed along with me. Finally, I just gave in and tore the paper open. When I lifted the cover of the plain pink box my breath caught. Nestled inside was a music box with a ballerina on top.

My heart thundered, and all of a sudden there wasn't enough air. I couldn't breathe.

When I didn't say anything, just stared at the music box,

Linc filled the silence. "I hope I got it right. I remember that you used to really like them."

My hands shook as I reached out to finger the delicate ballerina on top. "It's beautiful." I glanced up at his expectant face. "I don't know what to say. When did you get this?"

"Yesterday when you and Jilly were chatting. Did I get it right? I remember when you were kids, Jilly got you one for Christmas once. I also remember you used to dance, so I figured maybe a ballerina or something. If you don't like it, I can return it."

I snatched up the box and held it to my chest. "No. I mean it's too much, and you shouldn't have gotten something so extravagant."

He just shrugged. "I know how hard it is for you to come home. I wanted to give you something special so you'd remember it well."

Oh hell. Tears pricked my eyelids and I blinked them back rapidly. I was not going to cry. Despite myself, tears welled in my eyes, "I don't know what to say."

"Say you love it."

I grinned broadly before launching myself into his lap and wrapping my free arm around him. "I love it. Thank you. You've been great, and I know I was a bit of a pain in the ass the last couple of days and I'm sorry. I am really grateful to you." I sat back, the box still clutched to my chest. "Which is why I'm so glad I did a bit of shopping the other day for you."

His brows shot up. "When? And I didn't expect—"

I waved him off with a hand. "It's not anything big. But I asked Jilly what would be a nice way to say thank you. She made what I hope was a good suggestion."

"Still, you didn't have to, Nomi. I was happy to help. Besides, it gave me some time to hang out with you. Which is all I really wanted anyway."

"Would you shut up and just open it? If possible, I love giving presents more than I love getting them." I pulled a box from the bedside drawer and handed to him.

Linc stared at the box for a moment, then up at me. "Thank you, Nomi."

"No, honestly, thank you. You've been great and well, I figure I should repay your kindness for agreeing to go with me to my parents' house tonight."

"Don't forget you're already going to drinks with me at my folks' house, so this really wasn't necessary."

"Okay, fine, then look at it as a helping me love Christmas again present. I don't know. Just open it."

I bit my thumbnail nervously. Maybe I'd been too presumptuous. Maybe he wouldn't want it.

He lifted the lid off the box and his body went still. For several long moments thick silence hung in the chasm of space between us.

Unable to take it for much longer, I started to ramble. "I'm sorry if it's not what you would have wanted. You said you didn't do that anymore. But I remember you being really good, so I thought maybe it was a time thing. Maybe I could remind you how much you loved it like you reminded me last night that there are some things about being here I love. Is this okay?"

Linc held up the 50mm camera and examined it. Silently, he removed the lens cap, adjusted the lens, then snapped a photo of me.

Oh shit. I ducked. "Oh my God, Linc! What are you doing? I don't have any make up on and I'm pretty sure I'm raccoon eyed from last night. And *hello*, naked here."

He laughed. "You look beautiful. Besides, that sheet is covering more than your dress did last night."

I clutched the sheet closer to myself and put out my hand to keep him from taking any more photos. "You're nuts."

He laughed. "Maybe, but I'm also extremely grateful. It's been a while since I held a camera. I guess I've been looking for a reason to love it again."

"I know it's not fancy. Hell, it's not even digital, but maybe you can play around with it a little." She shrugged. "I don't know." I was unused to feeling unsure.

He tucked a finger under my chin. "It's perfect. Thank you."

"You're welcome."

"Now are you sure you won't let me shoot some pictures of you? I'm feeling inspired."

I laughed. "Absolutely not."

"Fair enough, then how about I thank you properly." He gently placed the camera on the bedside table and took the box from me.

"Lincoln Porter, you look like you have something no good planned for me."

"Oh, I think you'll like it."

I giggled. "You know what they say, talk is cheap."

He moved so swiftly, he surprised me; before I knew what was happening, he had me on my back and had worked his way under the sheet between my thighs. He kissed my inner thighs lightly and I squirmed.

He blew gently over my sex, and I slid my fingers into his hair, relishing in the luxuriant feel of it.

"Do you have any idea how good you taste?" To demonstrate, he lapped at me and moaned as though he was starved for me.

I clutched for purchase on the sheets even as I held his head in place and rotated my hips into his questing mouth.

Linc varied his strokes, brought me to the edge, then drew back, teased, soothed, and quieted the fever. When he felt the desperate tension ebb out of my body, he ratcheted the tension back up again, slid his tongue as deep as it would go inside of me and drew breathy, desperate cries from me.

The orgasm started in my spine, slowly rolled out, and hit every nerve, every cell, and every corner of my soul.

With a growl, he splayed me wide with strong hands and didn't relent; he applied the pressure just how I liked it. Even as I shook and my body shivered, he didn't yield. He continued to lick and stroke me. Linc pulled a response from me, marked me as his. He never let me forget what he could do to my body.

It was only after he dragged another sobbing release from me that he kissed my thighs gently as he moved up my body. He tucked my limp body against his as he nuzzled my neck. "Get some rest Nomi. You're going to need it. I have some big plans for you today."

14

NOMI

I tugged on the hem of my pea coat and Linc squeezed my hand. "Relax, okay? They're your parents and they love you."

"Yeah, sure. As evidenced by the fact they they've been to see me exactly once since I left for LA?" Not to mention my mind wasn't in it. What I wanted to be doing was tracking down Nolan Polk, private collector. We'd met with a rep from the auction committee earlier today, thanks to Linc pulling some strings. The lovely man didn't mind our disturbance on the holiday as he was Buddhist.

But alas, no luck. I'd even tried the investigator *Sassy* had originally sent, I poured over his files, but still had gotten anywhere. "Sorry. I still have work on my mind."

"I can help you with that." He kissed my forehead. "Deep breath."

Easy for him to say; drinks at his parents' house had been easy enough. His father was having a lucid day, so he'd remembered me. They'd all had a great time, and Linc had looked really happy. I slid him a glance and tried not to think about how much it would hurt to leave him behind.

My mother was the one who opened the door. With her hair up in a French twist and a simple green knit sweater dress that looked great against her chestnut skin, she looked youthful. "Naomi, I'm glad you came. I—" She faltered when she saw Linc. "Oh, Lincoln." Then she looked back and forth between us and understanding dawned.

I suppose I should have felt bad about springing Linc on her like this, but honestly, I needed the buffer. "You said to bring him. That's okay, right? We were just at his parents' for their annual Christmas fete."

My mother recovered quickly. "Of course. Come on in. How are you, Linc?"

Mom slipped into hostess mode easily and gave him an easy hug.

He hugged her back and I couldn't help but feel a little senti-mental. If I'd lived another life, this could be a normal occur-rence, dinner at my parents' house with Linc. *Just for play. Do. Not. Get. Attached.*

The moment we stepped inside my parent's house, the familiar smells assailed me, the smell of the fire in the fireplace, the slight scent of cigars if I angled toward the study.

The pristine living room of course smelled like potpourri. I hadn't been home in eight years and the room looked exactly as when I left. When I'd been a kid, I'd made it a point to go in there to read or study just so the room got used.

Linc and my mother carried the brunt of the conversation as we made our way to the kitchen. The smells of roasted chicken and herb crusted potatoes wafted out to greet us.

My father grinned when he saw me and wiped his hands on a spare dishtowel after dropping the spoon into the pot. "How's my baby girl?" His bright white smile a contrast to his ebony skin.

I blinked in confusion. I hadn't talked to them in weeks. I

normally spoke to them maybe once a month. And over the last eight years I'd seen them once in LA. They'd made excuses any other time I invited them. "I've missed you, baby." Awkwardly, I returned the hug, though it probably ended up looking like a flailing seal impression. I managed to mumble an appropriate response.

When he released me, he studied me closely. "You look too thin. Don't worry about that though. I'll make sure you fatten up before you go back." Dad had always been the one to do the cooking.

It was only then that my father noticed Linc, and his brows snapped down. "Lincoln? What are you doing here?"

Linc didn't even seem phased as he came to shake his hand. "Mr. Adams, good to see you again."

"I invited him, Dad. We ran into each other at the Porter's, and I thought it would be nice." Okay, small fib, but it sure beat, 'We're having a fling, Dad.'

My father looked unconvinced, but still he shook hands with Linc. As we all sat down to dinner, topics stayed light. They peripherally talked about my job and what I was doing back in Faith. All of it, conversations that could be had with a stranger, which in essence, I was. Linc knew more about my life now than they did.

It wasn't until Linc excused himself to take a call from his mother that shit got real. He squeezed my knee under the table, but the moment he let go, I felt oddly adrift and alone. In the span of days a feeling I'd long been acquainted with had become uncomfortable.

My father started first. "Sweetheart, I don't want to pry, but is it really wise to take up with the Porter boy?"

My mother groaned. "Charles, don't start. We just got her home."

"Take up with?"

"We weren't born yesterday. I see the looks between you two."

"Linc is a friend, Dad. I'll be going back to LA as soon as I do what I came to do."

My mother frowned. "So that's it, you'll just run back, and we won't see you again?"

I didn't miss the jibe. "You know where I am. I've encouraged you to visit often. You've come once."

The muscle in my father's jaw ticked. "Isn't this how we ended up here? You picking the wrong boy and not listening to us."

My blood simmered to life. "I picked the wrong guy once. I was a kid and naive. And because of that you punished me. You let me be humiliated. No matter what, I'm your daughter. It's your job to protect me."

"We tried that before, remember? You don't listen. You do what you want anyway."

"When are you going to stop punishing me for that, Daddy? I was a kid. I didn't know any better. But you're still my father. No matter what, you're supposed to keep fighting for me."

My father threw down his napkin. "What do you call uprooting you from that school and moving you here? Your mother was lucky to get the job she got. I was lucky to find a teaching position in the school. And what do you do? You go and slide back into a relationship with the exact same kind of boy that got you in trouble in the first place. Repeating mistakes and patterns of the past."

I shook my head. "But that's just it. Brad wasn't Jacob. Sure, he wasn't a peach, but if you'd been paying attention, you'd have seen that I learned a little bit from the previous experience. I'm not a fool, except at the end when my own parents kept me in the dark."

"And if we'd told you, you would have dug your heels in and done what you wanted."

"So you thought, oh we'll show her? I'm sorry. I've said it a million times, but you can't punish me my whole life for a decision I made when I was fourteen. If that's the way you feel about it, then there's really no point in me being here. I don't need your approval or your love. I've made it eight years without it." I walked out to find Linc and didn't bother with a backwards glance.

\#

I drove aimlessly for thirty minutes before pulling into the drive through of one of the only open fast-food places on Christmas day. After taking a bite of her burger, Nomi moaned and did a little dance.

"Oh God, that's good. Or maybe I'm just that hungry." She shook her head. "I'm really sorry. I didn't want you to have to hear any of that."

I shrugged. I'd certainly heard worse. "It's the holiday. Lots of people are tense."

Nomi shook her head, dislodging her braids around her shoulders. "No. I knew it was likely to be a disaster, but still I dragged you along. I thought he'd be inclined to behave if you were there, but it seems that might have made it worse, if possible."

"I guess he's not a fan of mine."

"No. It has nothing to do with you at all. It's me. And his inability to see past any mistake that I've made."

"You want to tell me about the mine field we wandered into?"

Nomi blew a stray braid out of her face. She sighed before speaking. "So, you know how we moved here from Alexandria?"

"Yeah, when your mom got the job with my dad."

"Yeah, well, they got in the habit of telling everyone that it was the opportunity that brought us here. When in reality it was the need to get me away from a situation in Alexandria that brought us. Mom's job was just the means."

I waited as patiently as I could for any snippet she might share with me. I felt like I was sixteen again, waiting for a glimpse of the real her.

"So right before high school started, my class took a tour of the new high school that was built. It was on the edge of a more affluent part of town, so it was going to be pretty economically mixed. Mom was an aid for Congressman Jeffers then and Dad was a teacher at the school. On tour, I met this boy, Jacob; his dad played for the Redskins. But they lived in Alexandria. He was nearly sixteen and like cotton candy crack to a young impressionable girl. I wasn't even in high school yet and he put the press on me. He called all the time, wanted my attention, wanted to spend time with me."

I smiled. "Can't say I blame the guy."

She returned my smile tentatively. "Dad couldn't stand it. He hated the kid. Swore he was trouble. Said that I was blinded."

"Let me guess. At the time you thought he was being over-protective?"

Her laugh was harsh. "Uh, yeah. Just a little. I thought he just didn't want me dating, wanted me to be a little girl forever, all the usual stuff."

"So, was he right?"

She nodded slowly. "Unfortunately. Once I started school, I saw Jacob every day. I'd get out of a class, and he'd be there, but not in that sweet way of just wanting to see me, but more like in the way that he wanted to make sure I didn't see anyone else."

My hands tensed on the steering wheel. But I didn't trust myself to say the right thing.

"Next thing I knew, he was suspicious of every single friend I had. He didn't want me going out. He didn't want me leaving my own house unless it was with my parents or with him."

"What did your parents do?"

"Well Dad could see some of it coming. Apparently, Jacob

had this girlfriend who'd eventually left the school. Her parents complained about harassment, but because of his father's connections everything was kept quiet."

"Guys like that are dangerous, Nomi."

She sighed. "I know that now. But at the time, I thought I had it right. Can you imagine a fourteen-year old me in love?"

Yeah, I could. And I didn't like it. "Did he hurt you?"

It was only when she shook her head that I marginally relaxed. "Never physically. But he had this way of belittling me so completely that I prayed for a kind word from him. He had me so completely under his control."

"What did your parents say?"

"They tried to talk to me. Tried to threaten to send me away to school. When they did that, Jacob threatened my father. Dad tried to have him arrested but nothing ever came of that. Finally, they decided to move. Dad lost his tenure." She shrugged. "All because of me."

"I doubt they see it like that. They love you."

"You were there. Dad sees it like that. He gave up everything because I wouldn't listen. Then we move here and inside of a year, I'd gotten with another pampered rich kid who thought he owned the world."

"I'm sorry Nomi. I guess seeing me tonight set him off."

She shrugged. "Not your fault. Mom did say to bring you. She always liked you. Besides, I'm here to do a job. When it's over, I'll go back to my life. I didn't come back here to patch things up with my parents."

A fist of cold dread settled in my belly. When she was done here, would she leave me behind?

15

NOMI

I felt like I was living in a dreamland. After the last few days spent with Linc and Jilly, I realized I was actually happy to be in Faith. That happy, glowy feeling evaporated, however, the moment Linc and I arrived at the country club for the wedding.

Through the ceremony, I could feel Linc's eyes on me, as he watched for any reaction to Brad. I hadn't really felt anything. Mostly boredom. If I ever got married, I would do it differently. I wanted it to be a party with real music and not some violin quartet.

From my position on the balcony I watched Linc brave the throngs at the bar in an attempt to get me a drink. I marveled at the way he moved. My breathing still hadn't returned to normal from our session in the limo. He had a sixth sense about how to touch my body and make me melt.

"Well, well. Look who blew back into town."

My stomach seized. That shrill voice could only belong to, Melinda Barnes. When I opened my eyes, I came face to face with the girl who'd made my life unpleasant in high school. The good news was, Melinda wasn't aging well. She looked like she'd had so much filler her face was frozen...and not in a flattering way.

"Melinda, I see you're still a bitch. Good to know things don't change."

Melinda narrowed her eyes and fired death-ray glares, but somehow I was less bothered by her now. "What the hell are *you* doing here? I know *you* weren't invited, as this is a society wedding."

"I'm Linc's date. I'm not here for you." I forced a smile and added, "What are you doing back in Faith? I seem to recall you telling us all the time how you were destined for greater things."

Melinda pursed her lips. "And I am. I'm just here in the middle of hell because Brad didn't have the good sense to have the wedding in DC. You're not here to try and get him back are you? So sad if you are."

"Linc knows that I couldn't give a shit."

Melinda paled, then darted a glace in Linc's direction, but he had his back turned to the balcony. "You came with Linc? Porter?"

"Not that it's any of your business, but yes."

Melinda's shrill laugh filled the deafening silence of the night air. "That is fantastic. I love it. You're here with my cast off? Let me break it to you, sister. If I can't get that man to commit, there's no way in hell he's going to commit to someone like you."

The darkness of the balcony started to encroach on my vision, and my stomach cramped as if someone had stabbed me in the gut. "Commit?"

As if sensing a weakened animal, Melinda moved in for the kill. "Oh, he didn't tell you? I mean after I helped build his career, he got cold feet. I'm the reason anyone even knows who Nolan Polk is."

No. My lungs constricted. He wouldn't have lied to me. Would he? For what? Why would he play games with me?

Breathe, mama. Just breathe. In...out. "If you'll excuse me, I'll just go find my date."

Even though the hot fire of betrayal had incinerated my bones and there was nothing to hold up my muscles, I made sure I held my shoulders stiff. I found him by the bar speaking to the groom and my body seized, then planted. *Fuck.*

Whatever. Big girl panties on. "Linc, excuse me, I know you're pretty busy, but I'm going to leave."

He grinned at me when he looked up, then seemed to register what I'd said, and his brows snapped down. "Are you feeling okay?" He completely ignored Brad, who had yet to turn around.

"No, *Nolan,* I'm not okay."

Linc's eyes widened imperceptibly, then narrowed. "Naomi."

Unfortunately for me, Brad chose that moment to turn around. Immediately his gaze skimmed over my body. "Nomi, is that you?"

"Naomi," Linc and I corrected automatically.

From what seemed like a far-off distance, I heard Brad's question. "What are you doing here?"

"Apparently being lied to. But I was just leaving. Good thing I know the way."

It wasn't until I entered the main courtyard while I blinked away a hot splash of tears, that I realized Linc had followed me. Okay, not followed exactly, as he was walking towards me. His breathing was slightly labored as if he'd run to catch me. "Naomi, listen to me."

I was not jumping on this crazy train. This was not my circus, and not my monkeys. "I have nothing to say to you right now. If you want to speak to me, we can do it at your agent's office in the morning."

"Shit." He ran both hands through his hair. "Nomi, I'm sorry."

"Don't you dare call me that." I jabbed a finger in his chest.

"That name is for friends and loved ones. You, are neither of those."

\#

LINC

That jibe hurt me more than anything. "Fuck! I know. I should have told you."

"Should have? Are you serious right now? You could have told me a million times. You *slept* with me. At any time while you were busy licking all of your favorite places, you could have told me. But you chose not to."

"Nomi, wait. Please listen to me."

Anger flashed in those warm chocolate depths. "Why would I do that? You lied to me. Please explain why I would want to hear anything you have to say."

Panic coursed through my veins. I couldn't lose her over this. I needed her. In just a week, I was already too close to her. She was under my skin. "I'm sorry. I never intended to lie to you. When you called and said you were looking for Nolan Polk you caught me by surprise."

"Oh really, because that would have been a fine time to tell me the truth."

"It's not that easy, Nomi. That part of my life is over. I haven't been able to shoot in years. Not anything worthwhile anyway. The camera you gave me, those are the first shots I've wanted to take in ages."

"You can stop blowing smoke up my ass." She shook her head. "God, I'm such a fool. I dragged you all over town. Was that cabin even yours?"

I had nothing to hide now. She knew everything. The one thing I wanted to know was, how? "Yes, the cabin is mine. I rent it so my name won't be on any of the documentation. I learned the hard way that my anonymity is paramount."

She didn't look like she believed me or cared. "Why lie to

me, Linc? You know how badly I needed to work with you. Instead, I've been chasing my tail around looking for someone who was right next to me. Do you have any idea how stupid I feel?"

I rubbed a hand over my face. "I'm sorry. I didn't want to lie, but then you were strutting around in full search and destroy mode and I didn't know what you wanted from me."

"Well, if you'd pull your head from your ass, you'd see that all I want to do is show your talent to the world and pay you handsomely for the privilege. I don't want anything else from you. Nothing."

I winced. I wanted a hell of a lot more from her. "I've been trying to find a way to tell you the truth since the party. I wanted you so bad, but I've been burned before."

Her dark brows softened slightly. "Melinda?"

I nodded. "She went to Carnegie too, and we started seeing each other at the end of freshman year. She took some of my earlier photos to a gallery owner she knew, and that was the beginning of my career. I went by Nolan Polk because I don't want my surname affecting my passion. I proposed my senior year. Then everything went to shit."

"Let me guess. Melinda isn't so much a gem as she is a thorny bristly cactus."

My chest tightened as I relived my past. "She officially became my manager my senior year at CMU. Things started to go bad as soon as I started selling to bigger galleries. Suddenly it was more about being seen at the right parties and with the right people than being with me. It was an ugly break up. And because I loved her, I hadn't paid close enough attention to my contract, which stated that except for charity pieces, she was due a cut of every single sale I made for three years."

Nomi's body sagged and she expelled a long breath. "That's why you stopped producing."

"My contract is officially over tomorrow. I can start selling photos again."

Nomi crossed her arms. "I see she's still bitter."

"Just a little. When you showed up wanting my work, I wasn't sure what to do with that. She taught me not to trust anyone and you were so driven I thought you would put what you needed before how I felt."

Nomi flung her arms out. "Linc, that is not me. We could have talked through your concerns. You know how I feel about your work. The whole thing should have gone something like this. 'Hi Nomi, long time. Which piece would you like?' I purchase. Easy. Done. Then you ask me out."

I stepped forward and reached for her, but she pulled back out of my reach. "Nomi, forgive me. I just wanted you to want me for me before you knew I was Nolan Polk."

Her voice was soft. "Why?"

I studied her closely. Needing to touch her. "Why what?"

"Why did you pretend to care about me? I mean, fine, it's only been a week, but you made it sound—" she stopped short.

Fuck if she didn't want to be touched; I had to make her understand. I brushed a stray tendril form her face. "Nomi, I told you the truth. I've been fascinated with you since you first showed up in Faith. And this time you were here and single and I wanted you to see me for me and not what I could do for you."

Nomi shook her head. "You only gave me part of you."

"I know." I traced my thumb over her cheek. "I should have trusted you. Please let me make it up to you tonight. Anything you want to know."

"Linc, I leave tomorrow. I don't think this is a good idea."

The tightness around my chest squeezed to a pain point. And I dragged in a ragged breath. "Let me earn your forgiveness. I know you're leaving, but give me the day."

She shook her head. "Linc—"

"Don't pull back. Not after what happened this week." I cupped her face.

"You lied to me."

"And I'm begging you to forgive me. I fucked up. I know it. Give me one more day to make it right. Stay."

I held my breath as she shifted from foot to foot. I could feel her emotionally pulling back. Could feel her distancing herself, and then she said something that surprised me.

16

NOMI

Three little words had me in full panic.

Just three words and I was off my axis and completely terrified.

"Okay, I'll stay." I had told him I'd stay. Knowing full well what it meant.

This is a mistake, the tiny voice in the back of my mind whispered to me. *You'll only get hurt.* No. I would not get hurt, because this was just for now. I wasn't getting attached to him. Especially not knowing what I knew now.

The drive out to the cabin was a dark and silent one. The tension in the car was thick and charged, with uncertainty, anticipation and remorse. Linc held my hand the whole way there, occasionally he squeezed it as a silent apology.

He led us into the cabin, and I smirked. "You had fun watching me play detective, didn't you?"

"Only a little." His grin was fleeting. "Have a seat. You want coffee or something while I get some of the images out of storage?"

I frowned. "We've already been all over this place; I didn't see any photos."

Linc shrugged. "There's a converted cellar. I had it renovated and made watertight. I use it as a dark room and storage."

A flare of remorse hit me square in the chest. I could see how after Melinda, he thought he needed to be wary of me. I'd been a little ruthless in my pursuit. "Linc, you know I wouldn't ever use you, right? I wouldn't ever exploit you."

He paused in his movement of the table to give me a soft smile. "I know you wouldn't."

I shrugged. "Maybe you don't. So I'm saying it at least once."

"Nomi, I know it."

The tightness in my chest dissipated. "Good."

He pulled out several boxes of contact sheets and slid them across the floor. "Wow, that's a lot to go through."

"Well, tell me what you're interested in, and I'll send you the files."

A chance to go through all of his work? Do not go all fan girl, do not go all fan girl, do not—too late, the giddy squeal escaped before I could hold it back.

Linc blinked then a laugh bubbled out of him. "I feel like I've got a groupie."

"How nerdy is that? A photo groupie. I've got to start getting into rock stars or something."

He laughed again and the sound rolled over me and warmed me from the inside. "I think I like you just the way you are. You make me feel like a rock star, so I'm going to hold onto that feeling."

We spent the next several hours pouring over the photos he'd taken over the last eight years. Exotic locations, familiar locations, some I preferred better than others, but the overwhelming majority I loved.

When we got to a set of photos he took in Angola, my breath caught.

Linc's voice was quiet, lulling. "This village, the women are amazing. It's made up entirely of women. They were fascinated to see a man, especially a group of white men coming to take pictures. All off their men and eligible boys have gone off to war."

Momentarily unable to speak around the emotion clogging my chest, I massaged the sore spot. "Linc, these are beautiful."

"All of them, they're really strong. They reminded me of you." He shook his head. "I mean, there I am in a far-off land, and I hadn't seen you in at least two years, and I was pretty sure you didn't know my name and I was thinking of you."

Wow, and what did a girl say to that? "Seriously, they're exquisite. I'd like to use these if you don't mind."

He shook his head. "No. Not these."

"Why not?" I didn't understand.

"These women. Their stories are really personal to me. It's part of why Melinda and I went our separate ways. She wanted to put a price on them, and I wouldn't go there. I'll share them with you, but I don't want these as part of the public sphere. They trusted me with their stories, and I want to keep that trust."

I nodded. "I understand. Thank you for sharing them with me."

"Is there anything else you want?"

"Okay, the photos you took of the South African university students going on protest. Then I'd love the ones in India of the Bollywood girls eager to be stars. And the ones from Hong Kong too."

"Done, they're all yours."

"Just like that?"

"Your wish is my command."

"I could get used to the sound of that." I dragged out my laptop. "Damn it, my battery is low."

"Okay, let me send the links to the files over to you, then you can do what you need with them. I'll attach my standard photo release too."

"Thank you. I'll send them over to my assistant. Linc, I appreciate it. It means a lot that you'd be willing to share these with me."

His voice was low. "I should have just told you. I've just been really burned before and it taught me not to trust anyone at all."

"You can trust me, Linc."

"I know that. I should have known from the beginning."

I chuckled as I put myself in his shoes. "If I'd dated Melinda, I'd be gun shy too."

"Yeah well. I made a lot of mistakes. I'm paying for those now."

I quickly sent a note to my assistant with the links to the photos Linc had sent me. *Ella, please download and store these on my server. The ones marked NP123, are for the photo spread. Thanks, girl. I'll be home in a few days.*

My screen blinked at me, and I groaned as I sent the message. "Looks like my battery is gone."

"Were you able to send what you needed?"

"Yeah, thanks. You've made me a hero."

"I aim to please."

I nodded. "Can I ask you something?"

He shrugged, even as he drew the curtain back to check the weather outside. "Sure."

"Why did you quit? I mean, I understand the contract situation, but you could have still been shooting. Isn't that what Prince did? Changed his name to some unrecognizable symbol to still be able to put out music?"

He shook his head. "Not the easiest question to answer." He scrubbed a hand over his face. "I know it sounds like bullshit, but I couldn't find my muse anymore. After Melinda and Dad, I felt sort of hollow inside. But then you turned up. Shook things up for me. From the moment I saw you at the train station, I wanted to photograph you. You had that lost doe look along with this irritating persistence. I miss it. More than I thought. You made me see that."

"Linc—" the lights flickered, and everything went black.

Linc cursed. "I think there are some candles around here somewhere. It's likely the storm."

I shivered.

"Are you cold?"

"A little." He slung an arm around me and electricity skipped up my spine. The need rolled through me. I was in a world of hurt if just a touch could make me feel like this.

Linc drew me close, encompassed me into his heat. He smoothed a finger under my chin and tilted my head up. "This is how I wanted our night to end." He kissed me gently and teased the seam of my lips with his tongue.

I sighed and gave him access and he licked into my mouth, coaxed and teased. My insides turned to fire as he deepened the kiss which made my insides melt and my muscles loosen and liquefy. In the far recesses of my mind a little niggle of a thought pricked at me. *Enjoy him for now, because soon you'll have to leave him behind.*

Linc nipped at my bottom lip, lightly sucking on it. "What's up, Nomi? I can see your wheels spinning."

"It's nothing," I shook my head to emphasize the comment.

"Then why are you frowning?" he brushed his thumb over my bottom lip. "Don't get me wrong, it's sexy. Makes me think of all kinds of things we can get up to with this mouth of yours. But I know something is bugging you."

I chose to go with honesty. "I'll just miss you, that's all."

A hint of a frown crossed his features, but as quickly as it appeared it was gone. "Why don't you show me how much?"

17

LINC

Bright sunlight slashed across my eyes, and I blinked awake. Groaning and rolling away from the offending light, I reached for Nomi, but even though her side of the bed was warm, she wasn't there.

Blinking my eyes open and sitting up, I called, "Nomi? You're ruining my wake up call by not being in bed." Chuckling to myself, I tossed the covers back and padded into the sitting room, but no Nomi. She wasn't in the bathroom either. It wasn't until I wandered into the kitchen that I saw her note. *Lights are back on. Ran to the Bakery down the road to grab us some breakfast. Seems I need to replenish my energy. Wonder why.*

She'd signed it with a heart and her name.

I couldn't help the smile that tugged at my lips or the warmth that bloomed in my chest. *Easy does it. She's not staying. She's not yours.* No, she wasn't, but maybe she could be. Maybe we could work it out. Maybe this didn't have to be some temporary thing. *Thinking like that will only get you hurt.* And it would hurt when she got on a plane tomorrow. I'd been mentally preparing myself for it since the moment I'd seen her again.

Shielding myself from the pain of watching her walk away, as I knew she would.

I glanced around the tidy cabin where I'd isolated myself, hidden away the part of me that still needed to see and explore and be free. But Nomi had brought it out of me again. She'd been home for barely a blink of a moment and already I was shooting again. I itched to have my camera in my hands. Itched to capture the beauty in things. A part of me that I'd shut off to do what I thought I had to do. Maybe that had been a mistake.

I shook my head to clear the thought. Well, I wasn't going to do that anymore. And when she got back, we were going to talk about what would happen with us, because I didn't want to let her go.

In record time, I tidied up the bedroom and grabbed a shower, letting the hot water sluice over well-used muscles. I grinned to myself as I thought of just how well I'd used them. Being with Nomi was like being with a live wire. She said the first thing that came to her mind. And completely lacked any kind of filter. She laughed with her whole body and threw herself into every single emotion. *When had I become such a sap?*

Problem was, merely thinking about her made my body tight. Itchy, desperate. My cock lengthened against my thigh and as I soaped myself up, my brain conjured up images of her on her knees, sucking me deep.

Hell. I reached over to the dial and turned the water to frigid before I could get carried away. I'd rather have the real thing. Once I was dressed, I grabbed my laptop and booted it up. I scanned and discarded the usual emails. But one from my agent caught my eye. Subject: *So Glad You Changed your Mind.*

When I opened it up, my stomach pitched.

Linc, I'm so glad you changed your mind about this. I got the proofs first thing this morning. And they look great. They must have worked overnight to get these up. I've always said this was your best work. I went ahead and signed the contract since you've already given the release. Call me when you get this. Since obviously you're ready to work again, I have some other opportunities to go over with you.

I pulled up the proofs. A little voice in the back of my skull told me not to look. But I couldn't help myself.

Instead of the photos we had selected together, she'd used the images from Angola. The pain cut through my chest swiftly. She'd gone behind my back.

\#

NOMI

"Hi honey, I'm home," I called out, but there was no response. I dropped the bag of bakery goodness on the kitchen table. "Linc, are you here?"

After a quick check of the bedroom and the cellar, I realized he wasn't anywhere in the cabin. But it wasn't until I checked the living room that I saw his note stuck with a post it on his laptop.

I thought we had a deal. Took a cab back. Leave the car at Jilly's when you're done.

My stomach cramped. He'd left me. Abandoned me. I forced myself to take several deep breaths while my rational brain took over. I tried to file away the pain of being ditched.

I snatched the post it off the laptop and crumpled it. The motion activated the laptop screen and bile rose in my throat. "Oh God." *Ohgodogodohgod.* "No, no, no." The image of the woman from Angola stared back at me with her hauntingly beautiful eyes. Under the heading of *Sassy Magazine*.

My brain finally came online, and I sprang into action. *This had to be a mistake.* It was a mistake. I hadn't approved those photos. I'd sent them to Ella to put on the server and told her which ones to use. This wasn't supposed to happen.

When rummaging in my purse didn't produce the results I

wanted, I tossed the entire contents on the kitchen table sending lipstick, keys, my wallet, and bobby pins flying. I snatched up my phone and dialed quickly. Brianna answered on the first ring.

"Nomi, I must say, when you say you're going to deliver, you're not kidding."

"Brianna, we need to pull those photos. Those aren't the ones we're meant to use."

"What do you mean pull them? The mocks have already been sent and approved. The issue is supposed to ship in a week. I'm not pulling the images. What's wrong with you? You do realize that the whole point of you going into the belly of the beast, as you put it, was to get these images?"

I massaged my temples. "Yes, I know, but the wrong images were used. I'm due back tonight. I was going to select a few different options. That picture was not for all eyes. It was for my eyes only. I gave my word."

"Sorry pumpkin, if you didn't want the photos up for option then you shouldn't have put them on the server."

On the public server? "What? No, I didn't. I sent them to Ella to my *personal* server. She wouldn't."

"I don't know what to tell you," Brianna said. "Amber pulled the images and selected them herself. She even gave you full credit for delivering on Polk."

That bitch. "Look, I don't know what happened, but she should never have had access to those. We are not even working together on this."

"Don't worry about it." Brianna said, as if she understood. "I know she's doing the whole riding on your coattails thing and wants to peripherally have credit. I know you're the reason we can even do this issue."

Damn it. I needed to find Linc. I needed to make him understand. Make him see. I wouldn't have done this to him. I cared too much about him.

Fuck, what a colossal cluster fuck. "Shit, Brianna, I really couldn't give a damn about who gets credit, what I'm telling you is I promised the photographer I wouldn't use those images."

"I'm sorry. We're going with these." She paused. "You can't be that upset. You pulled off this coup. Seriously, you're not going to quit over this are you?"

NOMI

With little regard to the snow and the sheets of ice, I drove like mad to Jilly's place. Twice I almost spun out. Once I almost rear-ended another driver. And more than once I fishtailed. But I finally made it to Jilly place in one piece. Too bad I bought it and fell on my ass the moment I stepped out of the car.

"Damn it to hell."

Jilly came out of the gallery half laughing. "Shit, Nomi, are you okay?" But she couldn't mask the humor under the worry.

I dusted off my legs as I attempted to get my knees back under me. "Laugh all you want. I'm actually here for Lincoln. Have you seen him?"

Jilly pursed her lips. "Nomi, I'm sorry. He came through about an hour ago; he's pretty pissed."

"I know. And it's a total mistake. I never would have betrayed him like that. I know what those images meant to him. It was totally a mistake. I never would have done that. I'm trying to fix it right now. Do you think I might be able to see him?"

Jilly sighed as she shook her head. "I take it that you know who he is."

"Yeah, I had that little revelation last night. Thanks for the heads up."

My friend winced. "Yeah, I'm sorry about that. He's my brother and I know what he needed was some time to figure his shit out. I hope you can understand."

"Yeah, I get it." I shook my head. "I'm not even mad about it. All I want right now is to fix this with him. Is there any place he goes when he's really upset? Anywhere I'm likely to find him?"

"You've obviously already been to the cabin. Sometimes he heads to the lake."

"I passed the lake on my way back. Please think Jilly. I don't want to go back with him thinking that I did this to him on purpose— that I would use him."

"Have you tried calling him?"

"What do you think?" I pursed my lips.

Jilly tucked her hair behind her ears. "Okay, obviously, you've thought of the obvious places. Maybe there is one more. Can you drive?"

"Yes." I gingerly reached for the door, wary of falling again. "Get in."

They drove out of town about ten miles to a small farmhouse. Jilly pointed out. "This was the house we lived in when we were really little. Mom and dad kept the place."

"I don't remember ever coming out here."

My friend shrugged. "Yeah well, there's nothing to do out here, especially for teenagers, who weren't necessarily driving yet; it wasn't exactly a hangout spot. But in this case, it works. Especially if you're looking for solitude. You can pretty much see everything from this spot. With us so close to DC at night, you can get a decent view."

I let Jilly lead the way into the house. There was a truck parked in the garage, and Jilly suggested he'd taken a cab to her place, then to the farmhouse with the truck.

Linc wasn't happy to see us at all. Despite his anger, his glare for me was hot and charged. With Jilly, it was completely different. "You couldn't keep your mouth shut, could you Jilly?"

"Sorry Linc, I'm a sucker for love."

Heat suffused my face. "Jilly, can you give Linc and me a minute?"

"Uh, sure thing, I'm just going to go inside and make some coffee."

Then my best friend was gone, and I was left with Linc.

"I'm so sorry."

He shook his head. "Not your fault right?"

"I wouldn't do that to you."

His brows snapped down, morphing his handsome face into a pale comparison. "But still somehow you did. I should have known better than to trust you. But I was so caught up in you."

"Linc, listen me. The last week or so I've been home—"

He crossed his arms. "You want me to believe that you felt something? That you feel something? Been here, done this already. I don't believe you. You said it at the beginning; you were here to do a job. Nothing more, nothing less."

I shivered and drew my pea coat closer against my body. "No, Linc. That's what I thought I was here for, but somewhere between you picking me up and taking me around and exploring the cabin and dragging me to that wedding and going to dinner with me at my parents and ice skating, I fell in love. I've kept myself apart from everything and you've forced me to open up and care about something again. You taught me to love this holiday again. It fills me with home and happiness to think about mistletoe now."

"Pretty words, Nomi, but then again, you're a writer. I would expect nothing less."

"Linc, please."

He shook his head. "You said it yourself. It's not like this thing was supposed to last anyway. Only temporary right?"

That last jab sliced through my heart. Tears prickled behind my eyes, and I blinked them away rapidly. *I would not cry. I would not cry.* So what if I cared about him. So what if I'd started to care about somebody. It's not like he was special. I'd replace him when I got back to LA. Didn't matter if the sex was so good I'd never need chocolate again. He was totally replaceable. *Nope, I didn't care.* "Fine. But you know the truth of who I am. You said it yourself. Listen to that truth. I'm going back to LA in the morning. You know where to find me if you want to talk it out."

"I won't be finding you to talk about anything."

I shoved my hands into my pockets and started back to the car. "I know." I said quietly as I walked back to the car, I refused to turn back and look at him. There was no way I was going to let him see me cry.

\#

"You're an idiot, you know that?"

I rubbed the back of my neck. "Damn, Jilly, not now, okay. I'm not in the fucking mood."

"Well, it's about time somebody told you to your face: you're an ass. A dick headed asshole who just let the woman he loves walk away over some stupid shit because he's afraid of getting hurt."

I couldn't help it; my lips twitched, "Dick headed asshole."

"Yes." She huffed as she jabbed me in the chest. "You've been pining after that woman since we were kids. I swear, if you weren't my twin brother, I'd freaking kill you."

"Jilly, you wouldn't understand."

"What? I wouldn't understand getting hurt? Have you forgotten that my fiancé left me at the alter?"

I winced. "Jilly—"

"I know you wanted to kick his ass as much as I did. It sucked the big one. But this is different. You're hiding."

My temper flared to life. "That's enough Jilly." We weren't going to talk about this.

"No, it is not enough. Nobody ever challenges you." She pointed into the now empty driveway. "But that woman, she challenges you. God, I remember when we were kids and she came around, I saw this version of you we'd never see unless it was just you and me together. Nomi had a way of drawing you out of your room, making you interact."

"Shut it."

"I remember that shy, withdrawn kid. The one who used to take these gorgeous candid photos of me and my best friend. I remember you trying to take care of her and making sure Brad stayed on his shit to treat her right." She inhaled deeply. "You think I don't know that you were the reason Brad was on time to that homecoming dance, because you offered to drive? You made sure he got there, even though he was already wasted."

Enough. I didn't want to think about the loser I'd been. "Enough, Jilly."

"No, not enough. You've loved her forever. Don't you think it's time you stopped being afraid and go after what you want? Yes, you got hurt, but enough hiding. Enough using Dad as an excuse not to go live your life. Grab the devil by the balls and give him a whirl."

Despite myself, the laugh bubbled up inside me. "Jesus Jilly, that mouth of yours."

She grinned prettily. "It's why you love me." She tugged her jacket down and studied me. "Now are you going to go after the woman you love or what?"

"It's not that easy." She didn't understand. I didn't want to believe in someone again to have her not be what I thought.

"Well, you have to trust somebody sometime, and Nomi cares about you."

"What she *cares about* is her job."

"She's driven and she made a great life for herself after she left. You can't fault her for it."

"And I don't." *Liar*. "But she'll always choose her job."

Jilly shook her head. "And you will always be afraid to take that step. You'll be the one missing out. At least she isn't afraid to be bold."

Jilly stalked out into the morning air and as I watched her, I wondered just how right she was.

19

NOMI

I tapped my foot impatiently as I waited for my train. All I wanted was to take the train to the airport and get the hell out of Faith, Virginia. In the last week, I'd fallen in love, had my parents dig up and pour salt into old wounds and then had my heart broken. I'd gotten what I needed for my job, but it hardly seemed worth it.

Linc would never forgive me. He would certainly never trust me again. I'd done exactly what Melanie had done to him.

He'd thought I was just in it with him for the photos, and the end result had been what he expected, even if the intention wasn't there.

I brushed my braids out of my face and secured them at the nape of my neck with a clip. I just needed to wipe this whole week from existence. I'd go back to my normal life. Work, home, work, home, the occasional date. All very surface. The way I preferred it. I wouldn't feel this kind of pain again. Because right about now, it felt like someone was pointing a blowtorch at my heart. And I wouldn't recommend it as one of my top five feelings of all time.

All I had to do was forget all about Linc. The way he touched me like I was precious, the way he looked at me. The way he tasted. The way he touched me like I was precious. *Stop.* He isn't coming for you. There will be no grand gestures. This wasn't a romantic comedy. This wasn't love. I could only count on myself for my own happiness. Even entertaining Linc as a possibility had been a mistake. One I'd pay for, for a long time.

And this time, I meant it. I was never coming back to Faith, Virginia. The personal cost just wasn't worth it.

My gaze flickered to the signboard as I willed time to pass faster, but unluckily for me, only three minutes had passed since I'd looked the last time.

An image in my peripheral vision made me think I was seeing things. But no. It was my father with his slightly loping gate. He wore his favorite jeans and a sweater worthy of the 80s, with a leather member's only jacket, looking like a throwback. I stood. "Dad? Is everything okay?" There was no way he was here unless something was terribly wrong.

When he reached me, his lips were set in a grim line. "Nothing's wrong, Naomi."

"Don't lie, Dad. You wouldn't be here unless there was."

He scrubbed a hand over his face. "I promise, Naomi."

This time, I couldn't help myself and I corrected him. "Nomi, Dad, I go by Nomi."

The flicker of his lips into a slight smile surprised me. "We used to call you that when you were a baby. Somehow as you grew, we lost it."

How bad was it that I didn't know what to say to my own father? I shifted on my feet. "What's up, Dad? My train leaves in a little bit."

"You didn't say goodbye."

Really? He wanted to criticize me? "Yeah well, you didn't exactly make it so I'd want to."

When he winced, I wished I'd held my tongue.

"Nomi, I wanted to apologize for Christmas night."

I blinked at him. "Come again."

He rolled his shoulders back and made it a point to meet my gaze. "I was wrong and instead of holding you and telling you how much I missed you, I pushed you away...again."

I opened my mouth then closed it. Tried again and failed. It wasn't until my third attempt that I managed words. "I don't know what to say."

His quick grin transformed his whole face, making him handsome and far less austere. "I should never have blamed you for what happened with that Jacob boy. It wasn't your fault."

My hands shook. "I don't understand."

"You've always had this spirit. You follow your heart and have your own path. Sometimes it gets you into trouble and as your dad, I should have been there for you emotionally to help you through. Instead, I was angry and resentful that you didn't listen. I wanted to stifle that carefree, independent voice you had."

In the distance, the train to Richmond announced they were boarding. "Dad, that's my train."

He nodded. "I won't keep you. I just saw you with the Porter boy and I lost it. I had planned on pretending the past didn't happen, get us back on track, but then you came with him and I thought you were in the old pattern again. I should have warned you about that Lennox boy. I should have chosen to talk to you about Jacob DeWayne. Treated you like an adult. I realize that the freedom and bravery you exhibit is something I've always wished I could do myself and I didn't have the guts. I lost eight years with my daughter because I couldn't admit it. I'm sorry."

Tears pricked my lids and I sniffled. As if I'd been doing it for years, I walked right into my father's arms and let him hold me. This was what I'd been missing. Family. A sense of home. I hadn't known it until I'd been forced to come back. I didn't want to be alone. It wasn't better this way. "Daddy, I have to go."

He smoothed a hand down my hair. "I know. But your Mom and I, we're going to come to California for Valentine's Day. Take a second honeymoon. See our daughter."

I swiped at the tears with the back of my hand. "I'd like that."

He walked me to my platform and helped me with my carry on. "Just remember, Nomi, we love you."

Uncaring about the free flowing tears, I took my seat and waved to my father as the train pulled out of the station. If nothing else, I'd found my family again. Now if only I wasn't nursing a broken heart.

I found my seat and settled in when suddenly I got a text.

20

NOMI

"Congratulations Nomi. This is a huge coup." Brianna grinned.

Then why did I feel ill? I kept thinking back to Jilly's text. *He's wrong. Give him time.*

Except he wasn't wrong. I'd betrayed him. It was a mistake. But the result was the same.

I held up the magazine and fingered the image on the front. It was a beautiful shot. I just wished it hadn't cost me the one person I'd cared about in years. Just like every other time a wayward Linc thought intruded into my brain, I bitch slapped my inner sap. Thinking about him would only distract me.

"It's beautiful. I'm really proud of it. I just wish we'd gotten it another way. One of the others would have been great too. I just want to forget about the whole week. In all, it turned out well and it wasn't as bad as I thought." Especially the parts with Linc. I involuntarily winced as pain sliced through my heart.

Brianna smirked. "So the devil no longer lives in Faith, Virginia?" I smirked. "Oh, he still lives there, but he doesn't bother me anymore. I had been holding on to some shit and once I let it go, I started to have some fun."

"Fun? Will wonders never cease."

"It's no big deal."

Brianna's laugh was clear. "Oh really? Aren't you the same person who offered to handle all interns this summer if I sent someone else instead?"

"That might have been me. But it was a figure of speech. Interns are truly terrifying."

Brianna snorted. "Yeah okay. But the only thing that causes an about face like this is usually love."

My heart squeezed. Yeah, love. I didn't know anything about that. *Yeah you do.* No. I didn't. Except, I missed him. They'd only had a few days together, but I missed him.

I missed cuddling in front of the fire with him and talking. When he'd made me hot chocolate and taken care of me after I'd bruised my damned tailbone. He was sweet. And the way he'd told me that I'd been all he thought about when we were kids. Why the hell had I never seen that?

If I'd known or seen him, well, things might have been different. I would have stayed. And maybe not be sitting here now.

Brianna studied me intently. "So there *is* a guy?"

"Huh? What? Don't be ridiculous," I sputtered

My friend leaned forward. "Is it the photographer?"

Hell, how did I answer this? "It's an old friend. Things got a little complicated."

"Nothing like a little holiday distraction to chase always the blues."

"Yeah, I guess." And that's all it was. *You're the idiot who got attached.* Only to find out that he didn't trust me and placed me in the same category as Melanie.

"Uh oh, did you go and catch a case of feelings?"

I shook my head. "Even if I did, he didn't. So, that's all that matters."

"What if he said he'd been a total dick headed asshole?"

I whirled to find Linc lounging in the doorway to my office.

"Thanks Brianna, I appreciate it," He said.

I turned to find my boss grinning and shrugging. "What can I say? I'm a sucker for love. I'll go ahead and leave you two alone."

Once Brianna left, I was left alone with Linc in my office. His eyes went to the magazine on the desk immediately and my stomach roiled. But hell if I was going to apologize to him again. "What do you want, Linc?"

He sighed. "I knew this wasn't going to be easy. It seems I keep fucking up with you."

I crossed my arms over my chest and Linc's gaze hovered in the direction of my breasts for the breadth of a second. That's right buddy, look at them and weep. "You made it clear that you didn't trust me or believe in me. You lie to me, I forgive you. There's a misunderstanding and you refuse to trust in me. You thought I was capable of hurting you."

"It was easier to push you away than accept that I love you."

My breath caught in my lungs and strangled me. "What?"

He leveled a gaze on me. "I said I love you."

"That's nuts." I shook my head.

"You are obstinate and determined and kind, and vulnerable and fun and that mouth of yours, drives me crazy. I was an idiot to not trust you. I've been a little in love with you since you rolled into town, kicking ass and taking names. I knew you were unstoppable when you took your life into your own hands at seventeen and followed your dream. I don't deserve you. Please forgive me. I'm begging you for a second chance."

"Linc..."

He pulled me into his arms. "Shit, a third chance. I'm a little slow on the up take, but I get it now. I'm never letting you walk out of my life again. I love you. I *need* you in my life."

"My life if here. Can you handle that?"

"Funniest thing. I'm a photographer, so apparently, I can work from anywhere. And I want to be with you."

Relief washed through me. "I'm not very good at relationships, you know."

He smirked. "Don't worry, we'll fumble around in the dark together. As long as we have some mistletoe, we'll be okay."

"I'm serious, Linc; this love thing is foreign to me, and I'll screw up."

He grinned. "Love thing, huh."

I met his gaze directly. "Yes, I love you, Lincoln Porter."

"Good. It'll make living with me a whole lot easier."

Want more Linc? Click here!

~

Thank you for reading *MISTLETOE KISSES!*

I hope you're ready for my next wild ride! My Rogues just get sexier from here!

First rule of being a Rogue, hide in plain sight. Second rule of being a Rogue, never get involved, the mission above all.
But less than forty-eight hours on my new assignment and I'm ready to break every rule in the book.
Lissa Montgomery, the one woman I cannot tough or fantasize about.

Read about Nissa and Rook in ——>THE ROOK!

WHILE YOU WAIT, dive in to Liv and Ben's story with **The See No Evil Trilogy:**

It began with a stolen **almost-kiss.**
And ended in **revenge.**

She was never supposed to cross my path.
She was never supposed to know about the oaths I swore or the
secrets I keep.

But like a thief in the night, she **took my heart and ran...** even if
she wasn't mine to possess.
As a member of the billionaire Elite, I live by simple tenets. A
gentleman above all. Loyalty is everything.. Secrets whispered
are never revealed. And power is king.

→ Yes, you can pick up **Big Ben, The Benefactor** and **For Her
Benefit** now!

> *"...a dramatic, suspenseful and amazing read that*
> *you just can't put down. I loved it!"*
> ————**Goodreads Reviewer**

Can't get enough royals? Meet a cocky, billionaire prince that
goes undercover in **Cheeky Royal!**

He's a prince with a secret to protect. The last distraction he can
afford is his gorgeous as sin new neighbor.

His secrets could get them killed, but still, he can't stay away...
Read Cheeky Royal Now!

Turn the page for an excerpt from Cheeky Royal...

UPCOMING BOOKS

**THE ROOK
THE SPY
THE VILLAIN**

ALSO FROM NANA MALONE

CHEEKY ROYAL

"You make a really good model. I'm sure dozens of artists have volunteered to paint you before."

He shook his head. "Not that I can recall. Why? Are you offering?"

I grinned. "I usually do nudes." Why did I say that? It wasn't true. Because you're hoping he'll volunteer as tribute.

He shrugged then reached behind his back and pulled his shirt up, tugged it free, and tossed it aside. "How is this for nude?"

Fuck. Me. I stared for a moment, mouth open and looking like an idiot. Then, well, I snapped a picture. Okay fine, I snapped several. "Uh, that's a start."

He ran a hand through his hair and tussled it, so I snapped several of that. These were romance-cover gold. Getting into it, he started posing for me, making silly faces. I got closer to him, snapping more close-ups of his face. That incredible face.

Then suddenly he went deadly serious again, the intensity in his eyes going harder somehow, sharper. Like a razor. "You look nervous. I thought you said you were used to nudes."

I swallowed around the lump in my throat. "Yeah, at school whenever we had a model, they were always nude. I got used to it."

He narrowed his gaze. "Are you sure about that?"
Shit. He could tell. "Yeah, I am. It's just a human form. Male. Female. No big deal."

His lopsided grin flashed, and my stomach flipped. Stupid traitorous body...and damn him for being so damn good looking. I tried to keep the lens centered on his face, but I had to get several of his abs, for you know...research.
But when his hand rubbed over his stomach and then slid to the button on his jeans, I gasped, "What are you doing?"
"Well, you said you were used doing nudes. Will that make you more comfortable as a photographer?"

I swallowed again, unable to answer, wanting to know what he was doing, how far he would go. And how far would I go?

The button popped, and I swallowed the sawdust in my mouth. I snapped a picture of his hands.

Well yeah, and his abs. So sue me. He popped another button, giving me a hint of the forbidden thing I couldn't have. I kept snapping away. We were locked in this odd, intimate game of chicken. I swung the lens up to capture his face. His gaze was slightly hooded. His lips parted... turned on. I stepped back a step to capture all of him. His jeans loose, his feet bare. Sitting on the stool, leaning back slightly and giving me the sex face, because that's what it was—God's honest truth—the sex face. And I was a total goner.

"You're not taking pictures, Len." His voice was barely above a whisper.

"Oh, sorry." I snapped several in succession. Full body shots, face shots, torso shots. There were several torso shots. I wanted to fully capture what was happening.

He unbuttoned another button, taunting me, tantalizing me. Then he reached into his jeans, and my gaze snapped to meet his. I wanted to say something. Intervene in some way...help maybe...ask him what he was doing. But I couldn't. We were locked in a game that I couldn't break free from. Now I wanted more. I wanted to know just how far he would go.

Would he go nude? Or would he stay in this half-undressed state, teasing me, tempting me to do the thing that I shouldn't do?

I snapped more photos, but this time I was close. I was looking down on him with the camera, angling so I could see his perfectly sculpted abs as they flexed. His hand was inside his jeans. From the bulge, I knew he was touching himself. And then I snapped my gaze up to his face.

Sebastian licked his lip, and I captured the moment that tongue met flesh.

Heat flooded my body, and I pressed my thighs together to abate the ache. At that point, I was just snapping photos, completely in the zone, wanting to see what he might do next.

"Len..."

"Sebastian." My voice was so breathy I could barely get it past my lips.

"Do you want to come closer?"

"I--I think maybe I'm close enough?"

His teeth grazed his bottom lip. "Are you sure about that? I have another question for you."

I snapped several more images, ranging from face shots to shoulders, to torso. Yeah, I also went back to the hand-around-his-dick thing because...wow. "Yeah? Go ahead."

"Why didn't you tell me about your boyfriend 'til now?"

Oh shit. "I—I'm not sure. I didn't think it mattered. It sort of feels like we're supposed to be friends." Lies all lies.

He stood, his big body crowding me. "Yeah, friends..."

I swallowed hard. I couldn't bloody think with him so close. His scent assaulted me, sandalwood and something that was pure Sebastian wrapped around me, making me weak. Making me tingle as I inhaled his scent. Heat throbbed between my thighs, even as my knees went weak. "Sebastian, wh—what are you doing?"

"

Proving to you that we're not friends. Will you let me?"

He was asking my permission. I knew what I wanted to say. I understood what was at stake. But then he raised his hand and traced his knuckles over my cheek, and a whimper escaped.

His voice went softer, so low when he spoke, his words were more like a rumble than anything intelligible. "Is that you telling me to stop?"

Seriously, there were supposed to be words. There were. But somehow I couldn't manage them, so like an idiot I shook my head.

His hand slid into my curls as he gently angled my head. When he leaned down, his lips a whisper from mine, he whispered, "This is all I've been thinking about."

Read Cheeky Royal Now!

NANA MALONE READING LIST

Looking for a few Good Books? Look no Further

FREE
Shameless
Before Sin
Cheeky Royal
Protecting the Heiress
Big Ben
The Heir

Gentlemen Rogues
The Heir
The King
The Saint
The Rook
The Spy
The Villain

Royals
Royals Undercover

Cheeky Royal
Cheeky King

<u>Royals Undone</u>
Royal Bastard
Bastard Prince

<u>Royals United</u>
Royal Tease
Teasing the Princess

<u>Royal Elite</u>

The Heiress Duet

Protecting the Heiress
Tempting the Heiress

The Prince Duet
Return of the Prince
To Love a Prince

The Bodyguard Duet
Bodyguard to the Billionaire
The Billionaire's Secret

<u>London Royals</u>

London Royal Duet
London Royal
London Soul

Playboy Royal Duet

Royal Playboy
Playboy's Heart

London Lords
See No Evil
Big Ben
The Benefactor
For Her Benefit

Hear No Evil
East End
East Bound
Fall of East

To Catch a Thief

Speak No Evil
London Bridge
Bridge of Lies
Broken Bridge

The Donovans Series
Come Home Again (Nate & Delilah)
Love Reality (Ryan & Mia)
Race For Love (Derek & Kisima)
Love in Plain Sight (Dylan and Serafina)
Eye of the Beholder – (Logan & Jezzie)
Love Struck (Zephyr & Malia)

London Billionaires Standalones
Mr. Trouble (Jarred & Kinsley)
Mr. Big (Zach & Emma)
Mr. Dirty(Nathan & Sophie)

The Shameless World

Shameless
Shameless
Shameful
Unashamed

Force
Enforce

Deep
Deeper

Before Sin
Sin
Sinful

Brazen
Still Brazen

The Player
Bryce
Dax
Echo
Fox
Ransom
Gage

The In Stilettos Series
Sexy in Stilettos (Alec & Jaya)
Sultry in Stilettos (Beckett & Ricca)
Sassy in Stilettos (Caleb & Micha)
Strollers & Stilettos (Alec & Jaya & Alexa)

<u>Seductive in Stilettos (Shane & Tristia)</u>
<u>Stunning in Stilettos (Bryan & Kyra)</u>

~~~

In Stilettos Spin off
<u>Tempting in Stilettos (Serena & Tyson)</u>
<u>Teasing in Stilettos (Cara & Tate)</u>
<u>Tantalizing in Stilettos (Jaggar & Griffin)</u>

Love Match Series
*Game Set Match (Jason & Izzy)
Mismatch (Eli & Jessica)
~~~

ABOUT NANA MALONE

USA Today and Wall Street Journal Best Seller, Nana Malone's love of all things romance and adventure started with a tattered romantic suspense she "borrowed" from her cousin.

It was a sultry summer afternoon in Ghana, and Nana was a precocious thirteen. She's been in love with kick butt heroines ever since. With her overactive imagination, and channeling her inner Buffy, it was only a matter a time before she started creating her own characters.

Now she writes about sexy royals and smokin' hot bodyguards when she's not hiding her tiara from Kidlet, chasing a puppy who refuses to shake without a treat, or begging her husband to listen to her latest hair-brained idea.

COPYRIGHT

This is a work of fiction. Names, characters, places, and incidents either are the product of the author's imagination or are used fictitiously, and any resemblance to actual persons living or dead, business establishments, events, or locales, is entirely coincidental.

Mistletoe Kisses

COPYRIGHT © 2022 by Nana Malone

Cover Art by M. Malone

Edited by Nicki Spencer

Proof Editing: Michele Ficht

Published in the United States of America